M000027450

DEDICATION

*For my Mother and Father
your spirits are always
with me*

MICHELLE DOREY

The Haunted Inn

THE HAUNTINGS OF KINGSTON

By
Michelle Dorey

MICHELLE DOREY

ॐॐॐॐ

Copyright 2016, Michelle Dorey
ISBN: 9781519011633
Independently published
092216CS

ACKNOWLEDGEMENTS

I need to thank those who made this book possible. Although my name is on the cover, it's a labor that had been touched by many hands, eyes, brains and hearts. Without your help, this would be a much lesser effort: Brenda Murphy, Rick Gagnon, dearest Corliss, and of course my favorite narrowback Irishman, Jim have been invaluable in improving this book. I will be forever grateful.

And mostly to *you*, Dear Reader. Your purchase of this book and the gift of your time is something I treasure.

MICHELLE DOREY

<u>Contents</u>

MICHELLE DOREY

Chapter 1

Tim opened the door to the multiplex and stepped inside. Cheap night Tuesday was usually busy but tonight the line of people waiting to get into the screening rooms was insane. He took his spot in the lineup for the latest *Star Wars* installment and fished his cell phone from his coat pocket. His thumbs flew, and he fired off a text to Brad.

WHERE THE HELL ARE YOU?

Almost immediately, the phone buzzed in his hand.

**GETTING POPCORN. SAVE A
SPOT IN LINE FOR ME.**

He held his phone at his side and his gaze wandered to the people lined up for the other movie. What the hell? There were as many people waiting to see the *Haunted* movie as *Star Wars*? Sure the blockbuster *Star Wars* had been there for a week already but the *Haunted* one was totally kicking ass.

Why would anyone wait in line and pay to see something as dumb as a ghost story? Not him. He worked too hard to waste his money on silly stuff like that. Work! If you could call it that. It was an exercise in patience reporting to imbeciles running the accounting department. Imagine! Graduating with honours in Business Administration and putting up with that. There had to be a better way to make money.

Again, he watched the line for *Haunted* move forward. The profit margin for that movie had to be as good as *Star*

Wars, considering their respective budgets. That people would pay good money to see that...

His brain whirred in overdrive and his fingers flew over the small keyboard.

FORGET THE POPCORN! WE NEED TO TALK. I GOT AN IDEA THAT'S GOING TO MAKE US RICH!

Tim couldn't take his eyes away from the line-up. He was running a spreadsheet in his head, and as he calculated each column the more excited he became. He jerked around when Brad's elbow bumped him in the ribs.

"What's up?" Brad turned his head to see what his buddy had been gaping at.

"THAT!" Tim pointed at the other screening room. "Look at the people lined up there!"

The queue of people chatting, slowly ambled forward into the theatre. He turned and tugged at Brad's arm, giving it a shake. "Don't you see? Disney launches a blockbuster like *Star Wars* and yet that spooky movie still draws a big crowd!"

Brad shrugged and a sheepish grin played on his lips. "So? Sophie saw it yesterday and she said it's pretty good. People like that kind of stuff, I guess."

Tim felt like his chest was about to explode. He spun and this time both hands gripped his friend's arms. "We can get in on this!"

"WHAT? You want to make a movie?"

"No, but Disney made *Star Wars*, and that gave me an idea."

2

Brad dropped his head and looked at his friend from the corner of his eye. "You're losing me, dude."

"Remember when you were a kid and you went to Disney World?"

"Sure I do. It was a blast--."

"Well, my folks couldn't afford to go. Even now it still pisses me off!" He still had Brad by the shoulders.

Brad thrust Tim's arms away. "That was years ago! Enough with the whining about it!"

Tim leaned in with a smirk. "I'm not whining, dummy! I'm inspired!" He held up a finger and pointed at Brad. "You were down there for a week, and what did you talk about the most when you came home? What attraction really jazzed you?"

Brad shrugged. "The Haunted Mansion. I made my parents go through it four or five times." He looked over at the patrons entering the auditorium for *Haunted* and his eyebrows knitted together. Turning back to Tim he said, "What are you thinking, Bro?"

"I'm thinking a *real* Haunted Mansion!"

"What?"

Tim was so excited he felt himself shaking. "A hotel! Or a bed and breakfast! Someplace where people spend the night and —"

"And get the hell scared out of them!"

"YES!" What would people pay to actually *spend a night* in a haunted house?" Tim's body was tingling, every cell electrified and firing. Finally, they'd come up with something that could change their lives. No more being a

3

drone at the insurance company, over-worked and underpaid. They'd become *Entrepreneurs*!

Brad's hand flew up and pointed at the other cinema. "Holy shit! If those people are any indication of people shelling out good money on this kind of stuff... like Sophie for that matter..." He glanced at the ceiling and back, staring wide-eyed at Tim. "We're onto something sweet here, Bro."

"Exactly!" Tim clapped Brad's back and strode to the glass wall of doors. Laughing, he called over his shoulder. "Come on!"

Brad's feet raced behind him. He gripped Tim's arm. "Where we going?"

Tim grinned and tugged the door open, gesturing for Brad to go ahead. "We're going to do some quick research. Let's go downtown to the tourist section and check out that Haunted Walk tour."

Brad grunted. "I'm not going on that thing; it's dumb. You walk around the downtown area with a guide who tells ghost stories. Big deal."

"Have you ever taken the tour?"

Brad shook his head. "No. Have you?"

"Nope. But I want to find some stuff out about it." As he fell into step, he nudged Brad's arm. "You said it yourself. Sophie works retail, only making minimum wage, yet she spends a lot of money on this spooky stuff, not just movies, but books and videos, right?" When Brad nodded, he continued at full steam. "How many scary TV shows does she watch? Look, if *she's* willing to part with her hard earned cash, just think what we can get from people who actually *have* some cash."

4

"Yeah, you're right. Twenty-five bucks all in is a lot for her to spend at a movie." Brad's eyes were bright staring at his friend. "But, you know, I don't actually believe in any of that spooky crap—"

"We don't have to *believe* in it, man. We just got to make the illusion *plausible*! We can do this, Brad. The time is to act is now. We're young, ambitious, and let's face it, we're smart as hell. A *'Haunted Inn'*. I like the sound of it." Tim's feet hardly touched the sidewalk, bounding along to the car.

Ten minutes later, they were in the heart of the older section of Kingston, at the gathering point for the Haunted Walk of Kingston tour. A young man in a top hat and flowing black cape stood near a tall lamp post. A crowd of a dozen or so people milled around him.

Tim marched right up, flashing his friendliest smile. "Hi. You're doing the Haunted Walk, right?"

The tour guide looked puzzled for a moment. "Yeah? Are you here for the tour—"

"No. Actually...how many tours are scheduled tonight? How many people in each tour?" Tim edged by a middle-aged woman who was holding the ticket up, trying to give it to the guide.

The young man took the ticket and smiled at her before turning to Tim. "I do four walks a night. There's usually anywhere from a dozen to twenty people in each tour." He glanced over at Brad, including him in the conversation. "If you want to come along—"

"Not tonight." Tim sidled up to the young man and his voice dropped. "Do you mind if I ask you...what do they pay you to do this?"

The young guy edged back. "Twelve dollars an hour. Why? You thinking of applying for a job?"

Tim turned to Brad, the grin on his face shining in the dim light of the street lamp.

Behind him the tour operator continued. "Actually, there are three different tours, spaced fifteen minutes apart."

Tim's head spun and he did the math. That was almost two thousand dollars! And they did this every night!

"Thanks!" He turned tugging at Brad's sleeve. "Let's go get a beer, man. This is even better than I thought!"

"How much better?" Brad asked.

"So much, that I'm buying."

Brad stopped in his tracks and put his hand against Tim's forehead. "You? You're buying?" He shook his head. "This *is* a night to remember."

Chapter 2

Brad

The raven haired waitress set the two frosted mugs of beer on the table and flashed a flirty smile at Tim.

Brad's eyes flicked from her blue eyes to his friend's. Why were women *always* drawn to Tim? It wasn't like he was ripped with six pack abs or even all that tall. Tim's trademark was the smug grin and intense grey eyes. But women ate it up and came back for more, never giving a glance Brad's way. It made no sense at all; he was better looking than Tim *and* in a *lot* better shape!

With an embellished sway of her pleated miniskirt, the waitress sashayed away from the table.

Brad turned to Tim and scowled. "Don't even *think* of getting her number! I have to work tomorrow and for the last three nights, I had to sleep with the pillow over my head to drown out the noise from your room. Enough with the revolving bedroom door."

Tim rolled his eyes and once more that damned smirk was on his face. "Jealous?"

It might melt a woman's heart but it just made Brad want to cuff him upside the head. "No. I'm totally fine with Sophie, thanks!"

Tim rolled his eyes before leaning closer, his eyes once more bright and eager. "Actually, I don't care about that, at least not at the moment. It's our *idea* I want to talk about. We set up a haunted bed and breakfast —ten rooms, at two hundred a night. We'll make a fortune. Of course we'd have to run it twenty four seven ourselves but after a year or so, we'll hire staff and relax a bit."

Brad sat forward and nodded. "I don't mind working hard and I'm good with people. So basically we just need to find a haunted house and market the hell out of it." He snapped his fingers. "Hey! Maybe we can coordinate with the Haunted Walk!"

"Don't forget Fort Fright!"

Old Fort Henry was constructed when Canada was still a colony of Great Britain during the war of 1812. The massive hulking structure was created to repel invaders from the south. A military base, it was threaded with claustrophobic corridors and coffin sized sleeping quarters. Every October, this historic tourist attraction would transform into the foreboding citadel 'Fort Fright'. Where spirits of the long dead and recently departed would haunt its dank passageways. Spirits played by local thespians, but pretty scary nevertheless. And really, really popular!

Brad pounded a fist into his hand. "Holy cow, you're right! They line up for hours to go through that place in October!"

"Yeah, to get the shit scared out of them! I'm telling you Brad, a Haunted Inn would fit right in!" Tim grinned at his doggerel.

Brad looked out the window of the bar they were seated at to see another group depart for their Haunted Walk. He drummed his fingers on the surface of the bar and gazed around the room. Tir Nan Og Irish Pub was well over a hundred years old.

"Did you know that this place is supposed to be haunted?"

"What?" Tim darted his head around the bar. "Where?"

"I don't know for sure. Some girl who died in a fire or something back in the 1800's." Brad took another pull on his beer. "No big deal... but..."

"But what?"

Brad looked off to the side for a moment, pondering. "But... it's just that there's all kinds of spooky shit in this city." He waved his arm. "You got 'Fort Fright' just over there in the harbor, you have the Haunted Walk going great guns." He looked up to the ceiling. "This place is supposed to be kind of haunted, and a bunch of other spots in the city too."

"So?"

Brad shrugged. "I don't know..." He looked at Tim directly. "It's just that there's something about this city... that's kind of...." his voice faded.

Tim slapped Brad in the shoulder. "Kind of a gold mine if you ask me!" He nodded eagerly at Brad. "Yeah, there's something off kilter in Kingston, I'll grant you that. So our idea should fit right in, right?"

Brad was thoughtful for another moment. Yeah, it should. Kingston had a weird streak to it, no doubt about that. He just wondered if they should mess with that sort of stuff. He sighed. What the hell was the matter with him? Half of their marketing was already done just by putting the Inn in this town! He snorted and said to Tim, "What the hell, who ever heard of a ghost *committing* a murder, right?"

Tim rolled his eyes. "You don't actually give any credence to that crap, do you?"

Brad looked a little sheepish. "Nah... not *really*. But..."

"So cut it out! You're trying to spook me and it's almost working!"

Brad forced a laugh and let it drop. "Yeah, you're right. So what's next?"

"Well, we gotta find a haunted house, that's what."

Just find a haunted house? Yeah right. That might be harder than it sounded, even in an historical city like Kingston.

Tim's eyes were lit up and his words rushed out. "Look, I know the hotel business. I grew up with it at Mount Tremblant. As far as *buying* a haunted house, well... we can *create* one. As long as it's old and a bit creepy. Embellish its history or even invent one!"

Brad's eyes narrowed. Just because he worked in a federal prison, didn't mean he wanted to be a resident. "But...that's kind of fraud, isn't it?"

Tim snorted. "You think the people who pay to go on the rocket ship ride at Disney World actually *believe* they're going to the moon? I'm sure there'll be guests who'll question everything. That's normal. But, we make some spooky stuff happen with props. Believe me, the majority will get the experience they want. We're selling the sizzle, not the steak."

A Hollywood image of a ghost, an ethereal woman in a long white nightgown, the edges of her form blurred, flashed in Brad's mind. With the right lighting and the right actress, they could pull that off. Maybe Sophie could, play that part. It would mean they'd be together more often.

Haunted Inn...huh? His eyes narrowed and his fingers continued drumming the table top. "Remember my cousin,

Mike? He's selling real estate now. He was telling us at Christmas about all the rules and regulations in selling houses. I laughed at the time when he said they have to disclose if the house has a violent history or is rumoured to be haunted. But that could work to our advantage. Any house that's suspect, is likely going to be cheap, right?"

Tim nodded. "For sure. We should be able to practically *steal* the place." He took a long swig of the beer and his lips pressed tightly together. "I've got almost ten thousand saved. How much could you put into this?"

"Humph." Brad looked down at the table. How could Tim have salted that much money since working at the insurance company? Even with the better paying job working for the government, there was a lot less in his own saving account. "Eight thousand. We might have to hit up our parents for a loan, especially if we have to do renovations."

Tim shook his head and grinned. "No problem on my end. They'll be happy I'm becoming a hotelier, carrying on the family tradition."

Brad fidgeted in his chair and his chest felt light. This was sounding better and better. "We'll talk to the bank and see how much we need to have and how much we can spend."

Tim waved him off, his chin lowered to his chest, suppressing a belch. "You forget, this is my forte. I'll visit some mortgage sites, plug in some numbers on-line. We'll know tonight!" He chugged the rest of his beer and signalled to the waitress for the bill.

Her cherry lips curved in a slow smile, and her gaze locked with Tim's as she set the bill on the table. When she left, he picked it up and glanced at the back.

Brad did an eye-roll. There were a series of numbers scrawled under swirly script, 'Carly', on the small piece of paper. Of course. She'd given him her number. Poor little fool. She'll be just another notch on Tim's bedpost.

But Tim was too wound up to follow up on that, at least for a few days, hopefully. It was the only down-side to rooming with him, the endless parade of women and his total lack of shame about that.

Tim pocketed the note and fished a twenty dollar bill from his wallet. "Jeeze, I really hope we can pull this off. I don't know how much more of that place I can stand. My boss is such a total moron."

Brad wiped the froth of foam from his upper lip, setting the now empty glass down on the table with a thud. "Maybe we can see some houses this weekend. I've had just about enough with working at the penitentiary myself." He chuckled. "You and me? We're both trying to break out of jail!"

Chapter 3

Tim

They couldn't get back to their apartment fast enough. While Brad went to the kitchen for more beer, Tim grabbed his laptop and woke it up. He barely noticed when Brad set a fresh one on the coffee table and dropped onto the sofa opposite him, firing up his own computer.

"You check out the real estate, I'll find out how much we can borrow," Tim said.

"Duh! As if I didn't know. You're the finance guy, 'Mr. Trump'."

"Keep up the smart ass and you're fired."

It didn't take very long before Tim had numbers from two banks and a mortgage brokerage company. He let out a low whistle. This looked better than he thought!

He glanced across at Brad. "Three hundred big ones, Mr. Wilson."

Brad's eyes shone and his cheeks were flushed when he put his own laptop between them. "Shove over, Mr. Holland and have a look at these."

The logo of the multiple listing service was positioned at the top of the page, while below that were thumbnail pictures of houses, along with prices. When the cursor hovered over the picture, the specifications of the properties filled the space.

Brad's finger pointed to one on the top line. "Look at that. It's ancient. If it has running water and electricity, I'd be surprised."

Tim's eyes narrowed. That one was too run down, but what would you expect at that price? A house on the third line down caught his eye. Holy shit. It was a limestone monstrosity on a couple acres of land just out in the country. Wow. It was even on a lake. At just under three hundred K, it looked like a steal.

"That one." His finger touched the screen.

"Yeah, that one looks pretty creepy all right." Brad flagged it and then scrolled to the next page. There were a couple other properties that looked like they might be suitable and Brad flagged those as well.

Tim sat back and polished the rest of his beer off. "I think we've got a good start on this. I'll call an agent and see about looking at those houses on Sunday when you're off. We'll have to keep our jobs right up to the last day, so that the income's there to qualify for the mortgage."

Brad got to his feet and stretched, his long frame and arms almost reaching the ceiling. "We'll probably still need to float a loan from our parents. With the renos and covering costs until we can get guests... I think we'll need some breathing room."

Tim sat quietly for a few moments. He couldn't get the picture of that place on the lake out of his mind. There was something about it. If only it was as good inside as out.

Chapter 4

Brad

At six p.m. on the dot Brad pulled the door to the shop open. Immediately the smell of sandalwood incense filled his nostrils while the tinkling of bells announced his arrival. As always, the cluttered shelves, overflowing with everything from candles, essential oils, healing crystals to prayer mats and smudging herbs made him feel claustrophobic, rather than at peace.

Aphra, the fifty year old owner of *Quantum Leap*, looked over the top of her cats' eyes glasses and managed to grace him with a hollow smile. Her bony tattooed arms rested on the counter, a catalogue of some sort between them, while some sort pendant dangled between almost non-existent breasts. With the butch haircut, she made kind of an androgynous statement-neither ying nor yang.

"Hi Aphra. How's business today?" He inched by a display of crystal angels and prisms, feeling like the proverbial bull in the china shop.

Her heavy eyebrows were like caterpillars crawling higher on her lined forehead. "*Business*..." She inhaled deeply through flared nostrils and shook her head slightly, making the dark pyramid earrings flash in the light, "The cosmos is aglow with molecular structures, Brad." She turned back to the catalogue, easily dismissing him.

He stared at her blankly. What the hell did *that* mean? If not for the fact that she was Sophia's boss and Sophia needed the job, he'd say something smart, right back at her. Instead he just muttered, "Yes, of course." He turned and pretended to examine a display of copper rods set next to a row of books. A small sign below the display read "Divining and Dowsing For Water". That people actually bought into any of this shit was the real mystery of the shop.

"Brad!" Sophie's voice was cheerful, walking out of the back room towards him.

As usual, the sight of her auburn curls, the smooth ivory complexion and sparkling green eyes took his breath away. Her youth and friendly demeanor was in sharp contrast to her employer's reserved disposition. When she looked at you, there was a gentle curiosity and interest that made you feel you were the center of her world.

On top of her 'great personality' she had a killer body. She packed so much into her short frame. While Aphra was thin to the point of emaciation, Sophie was curvalicious. From the swell of her breasts to the flair of her hips she was utterly and completely all girl.

"Hi! Ready to go?" he said, tipping his chin at the door. He couldn't wait to get out of this claustrophobic shop and hold her close in the bright sunshine outside.

In answer, she winked and then turned to her boss. "See you tomorrow, Aphra. Be well." At Aphra's solemn nod, Sophie turned and followed him out of the shop.

Once they were on the sidewalk, he pulled her close and kissed her. The scent of her hair and perfume filled his senses. If not for the fact that he made reservations at the new steakhouse that had just opened, he would have suggest going back to her place and ordering in.

She reached for his hand and looked up at him. "How was life behind bars today?" Her mouth twitched in a teasing grin.

"Same old. You know, I don't actually go into the cells...I work with the Psychologist administering psych tests and doing data input." He smiled and squeezed her hand. Actually, going into the cells on the range might be more interesting than the clerical work he trudged through.

"Yeah, yeah. Better you than me. It's a toxic environment." She gave her head a shake and crooked her arm into his as they headed down the street. "I'd rather make less money and do interesting work in the shop."

Yeah, real fascinating work dusting the display shelves of pyramids and celestial crystals. It was a subject that they didn't agree on. He didn't get the whole mystical, quantum physics stuff and she didn't like to think of the criminals where he worked. He decided to change the subject before the evening got off on the wrong foot. In the three months they'd been going out, he'd learned she could be pretty stubborn.

"Hey! Tim and I are going into business together. I might be able to quit the pen soon if everything pans out." He grinned thinking this was something she'd get—the whole spiritual, ghosty thing.

"Really?" Her lips parted and her eyes were wide staring up at him.

"Yeah. We're going to buy a haunted house and make it a B&B. After seeing the market for spooky experiences, people wanting to get the crap scared out of them, we think it might make us a lot of money. And you know, Tim's family—"

She stopped suddenly and jerked his hand. "Are you kidding? That's crazy! Neither of you believe in the afterlife, yet you're willing to exploit people who do?" She shook her head, frowning at him. "What's more, this stuff is dangerous. You can't toy with the supernatural."

Watching her face contort, he felt the muscles at the back of his neck tighten. He should have known that she'd take the haunted stuff way too seriously. His voice was louder than he'd intended when he spoke. "C'mon, Sophie! It's kind of like the spooky house at a carnival, except that it's a hotel, a longer experience. It's not gonna be real! We're going to *create* the supernatural experience. We just need a big old house."

Her head jerked back, and she rolled her eyes theatrically. "Oh, that makes all the difference! You're just going to trick people and take their money." She yanked her hand out of his and folded her arms across her chest.

"You went to the *Haunted* movie. You paid good money. It was a story! People *want* the thrill. That's all we're doing." He reached for her hand, clasping her fingers through his.

Her lips set in a straight line and she stood silent for a moment.

This was a good sign. He kept his smile gentle, not wanting to lord it over her that he'd scored a point. "Look, how much different is it where you work? Whether the crystals, the candles or oils actually *do* anything is open for debate. But the people believe it and even if it's a placebo type thing, it gives them what they paid for, right?"

She let out a long breath and looked up at him. "But Brad, I'm worried that you may actually stumble upon a for real haunted house. Then what?"

There was no way he was going to push the envelope any farther. He didn't believe in any afterlife and so what if she did? It was sweet of her to worry about him. "I'll be careful." He put his hand over his heart. "Promise."

"Oh yeah?" She folded her arms. "How are you going to do that?"

Damn, this was starting to get out of hand. He cocked his head to the side and looked her in the eye. "You're really worried about this."

"Yes!" She stamped her foot on the sidewalk, and looked so damn cute doing it.

"Okay, how about I wear a garlic necklace strung together with sweet grass?"

"Brad this isn't funny! You're planning on messing with the astral plane and you don't realize what you're getting yourself into!" Her eyes were fiery now. "And making fun of me isn't helping!"

He held up his hands in mock surrender. "Okay, okay— I'm sorry for that." He lowered his hands. "Listen, Sophie, we're *not* planning on buying a *haunted* house. We're going to buy a place that only *looks* like it could be. We'll install some special effects or something to scare the guests, and that's all." He shrugged. "Kind of like the attraction at Disney World, okay? Safe as anything, and a real money maker, see?"

"Thanks for the apology," she replied. She looked away for a moment. "I guess I see what you mean," she said softly. Turning back to face him she smiled. "Although I'd love to see you wearing a garlic necklace." She took his hand and looked up at him. "It's just that this kind of stuff in the real world makes me kind of nervous."

At the smile blossoming on her face, he pulled her close and hugged her. He really, really liked her. Somehow, if they were going to last, they'd have to find a compromise on this subject. But, first off, he'd have to help her find another job. That mystical new age bullshit wasn't helping her stay grounded.

Chapter 5

Brad

Brad sat back into the plush cushioning of the front seat driving to the old house in the country. The real estate lady, Gwen Connors, had to be doing really well for herself. The car was a Beamer and she was probably only in her mid thirties. She had dark hair and although a little on the plump side, she was attractive and friendly enough. Her brown eyes were round and serious when she turned slightly, glancing at Tim in the back seat. She was sure taking her time answering the question.

"Yes. I'm afraid that's why the house is priced so low. It's been on the market for almost a year and the owner is seriously motivated to sell." She frowned. "There's not too many people who want to live in a house where a family was murdered."

"Sounds perfect." Tim's voice was a low murmur from the back seat, but in the quiet of the car, was still quite plain.

Gwen's jaw dropped and her head jerked around. She shot a look of consternation at him and quickly returned her eyes to the road.

Oh shit. Brad cleared his throat and spoke. "What he means, is that because of...well, you know, *that occurrence,* it's priced on the low side. Obviously, what happened to that family is tragic. But, it doesn't affect the house, not for us at least. We aren't superstitious, just poor."

21

Gwen kept her eyes on the road but gave a small nod. Following up, Brad continued. "So, this is your first time showing the house?"

She shook her head slowly. "No, I've had a couple of showings." She sighed. "But when I consider the amount of advertizing I've done, I won't do much more than break even when it finally does sell.

"Who owns the place?" asked Tim from the back seat.

Gwen shook her head. "I don't know. One of the lawyers in town put up the listing acting on behalf of an estate. Who the current owners are, and how long they had the place is something I don't know."

"Is that very common?"

"No, not really..." She started to say something else, but stopped herself. "Oh well, every property has a story, I suppose."

Brad watched her flip the turn signal on and the car slowed to turn onto a side road. They drove for a few minutes longer, passing by fields of green grass where a herd of cows grazed lazily in the sun. At a bend in the road, the sparkling, blue waters of a lake appeared.

"That's Loughborough Lake. The house is about fifty feet away from the shore, on a two acre lot." Her hand rose from the wheel, pointing to her left. "There it is."

Brad's eyes became wide gazing at the stately home...actually more like a mansion than a home. They drove down the narrow dirt lane, and he couldn't help but grin like a fool. The picture in the real estate site on line didn't do the place justice. It was two and a half stories high, made of limestone with tall windows, rounded on the top side. Green ivy clung to the gray stone, snaking by the entranceway to the uppermost point. If he actually believed in ghosts and spectral beings, this was a place where they'd want to hang out, all right.

"Holy cow." Tim's voice, soft and awestruck mirrored his own feelings exactly.

"Would you like to walk the property first or go right in?" Gwen's face was tight, and her smile seemed forced looking over at him.

Was she serious? He could hardly tear his gaze away from the stately manor. "I think we should check the house. I mean, what's not to love about this setting? Clean waterfront and a dock, a huge lawn and garage?" Brad pulled the handle of the car door and stepped out, taking everything in, from the small dormer windows on the top floor to the veranda wrapped around the ground floor of the building. It might be the first place they'd seen, but it was absolutely perfect so far.

Gwen walked ahead, crossing the veranda and opening the front door, a heavy, black wooden slab, the upper half a window dissected by swirls of iron grating.

Tim nudged him with his shoulder and his voice was barely above a whisper. "Pretty freaking amazing. I think we've found our house. The lake's an added bonus."

The creaking of the door hinges, wailing against the intrusion into the house, was like fingernails on a blackboard. Brad's smile fell from his face, watching the dark, yawning opening in the house and Gwen's pasted on smile. The fine hair on the nape of his neck tingled and he shivered, despite the warmth of the day.

Tim's hand landed solidly between his shoulder blades and Brad almost jumped out of his skin.

"Oops. Sorry about that." But the flashing grin from Tim was anything but sorry. "That creaking old door...Ooo, so scary. No way we're *ever* gonna' oil those hinges." He jerked his head to the side. "C'mon. Let's go."

Brad cleared his throat and with shoulders squared, walked toward the house. For a moment, he'd felt a little uneasy, but that was understandable. There was bound to be some hang-over effect of knowing the actual history of the house, some guy murdering his whole family and then killing himself.

On the positive side, they didn't have to make up some gruesome past. The house's history was authentic. That was something he'd have to keep from Sophie. She'd freak. He climbed the steps and crossed the veranda to the front door.

Gwen stood to the side of the door, extending her hand for them to enter first. She'd become more quiet and her eyes kept darting around, above a thin lipped smile.

When he stepped into the entrance, a musty smell filled his nostrils. Dust motes danced in the stream of light cascading through the high windows. Straight ahead was an imposing set of wooden stairs.

His back muscles tightened in a quivering shiver. The house felt chilly and the air extremely thick on his skin. He looked over at Tim, who was holding his elbows tight to his body. "Did you feel that?"

"Oh no, not again." Gwen's mutter drifted from behind them.

"Yeah. What the hell?" Tim said and glanced behind him at the real estate woman. "What was that, Gwen?"

She sighed and her voice was low, as if she didn't want to disturb the air. "Everyone who comes in here feels the same thing after crossing the threshold. My grandmother would have called it the feeling that 'someone's walked over my grave'."

Tim turned back to Brad and he grinned, "Bingo!" He raised his hand for the classic 'high five'.

Brad smiled, exchanging the feeling of dread for one of optimism and clapped his hand against Tim's. "Perfect!" He turned back to look around the foyer.

There was a curved archway on each side of the open space, and the light from the brightness of the day outside highlighted the hardwood floor in each room. He couldn't help wonder, where it had taken place—the murders.

Tim brushed by him, striding to the right, through the arched entry. "Look at the size of this room and that view. It's downright pastoral!"

Gwen sidled close to Brad. "It's a centre hall plan, with the living room on one side and the dining room on the other." She took a step into the room where Tim stood, gaping around at the walls and high ceilings. "This is the living room or as it was once called, the parlour."

Tim beckoned to him, grinning like a Cheshire cat. "I like that. The parlour. It sounds old fashioned. Come into my parlour said the spider to the fly."

Brad looked around, and his shoulders tensed in a soft shudder. The air was still heavy and he couldn't shake the feeling that he was being watched. His gaze switched between Gwen and Tim. "Is it just me, or does this room give you a case of the willies, too?"

Gwen nodded slightly, her smile now gone.

"It's perfect, isn't it? The atmosphere just oozes from the walls. I love it!" Tim grinned and rubbed his palms briskly together, his body fairly vibrating with glee. He spun slowly, taking in all of the room. "This just needs a good cleaning. No holes in the plaster or boards that needs replacing."

He continued, leading the way to the back of the house. "Oh my God, Brad. Look at this. Why the lake is so close, you can almost hear the lapping of the water on the shore."

Gwen looked over at Brad and her eyebrows bobbed high for a moment. "It *is* a lovely property." The tone and timbre of her voice belied the compliment, especially when she looked away so quickly.

Brad's gaze lingered on the realtor, seeing clearly her unease in the quick, strained movements and even her body language screamed discomfort. If her reaction to the house was any indication of how most people would be affected, they were going to make a fortune. As for his own unsettled feeling, it would go away or at the very least, he'd get used to it. He smiled and wandered slowly into the back room to join Tim.

One wall contained rows of shelves, floor to ceiling, next to a window overlooking the waterfront. It was bigger than the front room and much brighter, not quite as eerie. They'd have to work on spooking it up.

"This is obviously the library. We can raid old bookstores and get some ancient books to fill up the shelves." Brad chuckled. "And if some of the heavier ones fall, banging in the middle of the night... Well, that'd be great."

"Totally!" Tim grinned and pranced out of the room. His footsteps stopped and after a moment he called. "Brad. Give me a hand here, will you?"

When Brad got to the archway, Tim was pulling on a heavy wooden door that led to the outside. "I flipped the deadbolt. It must be swollen in the frame and stuck from not being used." He turned and smiled above cheeks that were flushed pink with his effort. Tim was the brains of the team,

26

not the brawn. The most exercise he ever got was walking to the fridge for a beer.

Brad rolled his eyes and stepped close, elbowing him out of the way while Gwen's voice sounded over his shoulder. "Sure, it's not locked?"

His eyes grew round and he lurched back suddenly when the door swung wide. He'd hardly used any force at all. It had seemed to float in his hands, opening to reveal a wooden step and flagstone path leading to the lake. The rush of warm air that flooded over him brought a smile to his lips.

"I must have loosened it for you. Honestly, the bloody thing was stuck when I tried it." A deep scowl dissected the dark line of Tim's eyebrows.

"Sure, Tim." Brad chuckled. He left the door wide open, letting the warm air from the outside flood through the house.

Gwen had left the library and beckoned them to follow her further down the hall to the kitchen.

"If you're serious about setting up a bed and breakfast, you'll love this kitchen. There's lots of room for cooking and you can see the lake and out into the greenhouse." For the first time, Gwen's smile was genuine and at ease, sweeping her arm while slowly stepping in a circle.

It was funny, but Brad also felt more comfortable in this room. For one thing it was bright, but not only that...the air seemed lighter. It was probably because the back door was wide open. Still, she was right about one thing. There was a ton of space and if the two of them were preparing a big breakfast for guests, they'd need that.

Tim looked over at him and winked before a long sigh seeped from his lips. His gaze flickered to Gwen and his voice became theatrical. "Yes. But the cupboards and countertop are dated. Kitchens are *expensive* to renovate. Too bad." Tim turned to face him, away from Gwen's eyes and grinned, before setting off to continue his walk through.

The bugger. Already trying to wheedle the price down. The corners of Brad's lips twitched in a smile, that he tried to hide from Gwen.

"The dining room, I presume." Tim called out, doing his best British accent.

Brad shook his head and wandered over to his friend. "Will you prepare the tea, Holland." He couldn't resist. They'd both seen too many episodes of Downton Abby that past winter and the fact that they'd found almost exactly the house they were looking for made them downright giddy.

"This is huge! We can feed an army in this room it's so big!" Tim was stepping on different floorboards, testing for squeaks.

A sense of sadness enveloped Brad as he gazed around the room. In his mind's eye he saw what it had once been like in days long ago. Over there a huge Christmas tree glowed with lights, tinsel, garlands and ornaments. To his left there had been a large dining room table festooned with turkey and all the trimmings. A family with small children were gathered around, joined by grandparents getting on in years. The blessing had just been said, and Father was about to carve.

In the wink of an eye it was gone. Leaving him nothing but a sense of cold, hollow emptiness. Not even grief nor fear nor terror. Just a sense of empty loss.

He sighed. He shoved his hands in the pockets of his jeans and turned away, gazing across the expanse of lawn to clear his head. Seeing the overgrown field, his eyebrows rose. That was another thing they'd need—a riding lawn mower. Well, maybe that could be fun.

"Check this out!" Tim's voice drifted from outside the room, from the open doorway and a brightly lit room. "There's a greenhouse attached to the house. We could have a small sitting area here and maybe grow some herbs. There'll be fresh flowers at every meal." He smiled, looking out the windows at the large maple tree. "I can't wait to show my parents this place."

Brad stepped into the greenhouse and took a deep breath of the pungently warm air. His fingers grazed along the shelf littered with chipped and broken clay pots, spindly dried up stems of plants poking from the dark earth. There was a desperate sense of abandonment in the room, more telling than what he felt in the dining room.

He picked up a broken shard of pottery and turned to Tim. "It's got real possibility, doesn't it? But, I'm not sure about the herbs and making this room all cosy and nice." Dropping the shard on the workbench he said, "That's not the point of we're trying to do here, is it?"

Tim, bounced the heel of his hand against his forehead. "You're right. I should be thinking of lighting and spectral images, not daisies and dill." He turned to go back into the dining room, but his foot caught on a wooden box jutting from under the shelf, making him stumble.

Brad, looked down, expecting to see garden tools or more pots. His head tilted to the side when he noticed the contents. A board game and some books? He bent and plucked the game up, dusting the top with the edge of his hand. The alphabet of letters arched over numbers one to ten, while in each corner were the words 'yes' and 'no'. Ouija? He froze, and a feeling of dread passed through him.

"Is that what I think it is?" Tim's lips parted and the look of wonder was soon replaced by a grin. "I think we found the creep factor for this room." Now it was his turn to bend down and pick the books out of the box.

Brad's eyes became round when he saw the titles. Oh my God. One was a Bible and the other contained an old man's face, set in a pentacle which in turn was enclosed in a circle. The word *Alchemist* as well as intricate scrolls covered the rest of the midnight blue cover.

Tim picked it up and leafed through the brittle pages. He looked at Brad with bobbing eyebrows. "Holy shit! This is gold!"

"What does it say?"

"Beats me. It's written in Greek or something." He held it up for Brad to look.

"That's not Greek; I think it's Latin," said Brad.

"Whatever." After closing the book back up Tim's finger tapped its cover. Some book about spells and stuff, together with a Bible and a Ouija board?" He nodded his head with a leering smirk. Perfect ingredients for spooky shit, that's for sure." He placed everything back into the box and tucked it under the counter. "I'm going to come up with some ideas on how to use this stuff." He held up a hand. "Wait a second! Maybe Sophie can come up with some ideas! She's into this sort of stuff, right?"

"Well... maybe. We'll ask her if we wind up buying the place." Brad's heart pounded in his chest and his hand that had handled the box tingled a bit. Tim was right about that stuff making some good props. Even so, it was unnerving finding them.

A rhythmic musical note broke the silence and Gwen called out from the dining room. "Sorry. It's my phone."

When Brad stepped into the dining room again, she slipped it from her purse and a look of relief lightened her face as she scanned the small screen. "I've got to take this. I'll be outside. You two just go on ahead and see the rest of the house." Her feet clacked quickly across the room, making her escape out the front door.

When the door closed after her, Tim's fingers clutched Brad's arm. "This is fantastic! I hope I didn't seem too anxious to Gwen. We've *got* to get this place, but as cheaply as possible."

Brad nodded. "Absolutely. She couldn't wait to get outside. She probably called herself on the phone for an excuse. I have to admit, a few times, I was totally creeped out, especially in the parlour."

"Me too! Isn't it great!" Tim poked him playfully on his upper arm. "This place is the genuine article if you believe in that sort of thing. If *we* sense it, imagine what *believers* will experience. Hell, we may be able to charge *five hundred* a night!"

Brad grinned and held his hand up for a high five clap. They were going to make some serious money from this house. Tim was right. And from what they'd seen so far, the renos wouldn't be extensive. His hand was still tingling, and Tim's high five didn't help; he shook it walking from the dining room towards the front foyer. Walking down the hallway bordering the stairs and noticed a door tucked under the risers.

He opened it and nodded. It was a powder room, with a white toilet and pedestal sink. It was obviously not an original fixture, but one that had been installed much later. Maybe by that poor family? His shoulders sagged and a long sigh hissed from his chest.

He shook his head and took a deep breath. No matter. It would save them the expense of adding a bathroom on the main floor.

He turned and backed out of the room at the thud of Tim's feet on the stairs above him. Now that Gwen had left, they could talk more freely. He gripped the banister and raced to catch up.

"Holy shit!" Tim's booming voice, bounced down the stairwell.

Brad paused for a moment. "What is it?" Without waiting for an answer he stepped quicker up the last few steps. At the top landing, about five feet away was another set of stairs, this one, much narrower. Of course, that one had to lead to the attic.

He turned to see Tim standing in the centre of a long hallway, staring at a window that overlooked the lawn and front of the house. The dark floor and the green art deco pattern of the wallpaper above the crackled varnish on the baseboards were downright gloomy. Even the sunshine that tried to invade the space was bleary from windows that were filthy and smudged.

"Isn't this great? The hallways on each side of the stairs and the window on the far wall? It's right out of an Edgar Allan Poe novel." Tim glanced over his shoulder at Brad and smiled.

Brad laughed and he muttered, "It was a dark and stormy night..." turning to push the first door open. Directly in front, on a black and white, marble tiled floor, was a painted vanity topped with a rust stained sink. At the far wall, was a white toilet, while an ancient, claw-foot bath tub claimed all of the other wall. A small window peeked high above it. Again the sad sense of abandonment and loss hit him as he backed out slowly.

"There're three bedrooms on each side of the stairwell. I know we were hoping for ten bedrooms but I think this will work." Tim opened the door to the first bedroom and disappeared inside.

The musty smell he'd noticed when he'd first set foot in the house was stronger up, as well as kind of clammy. He started breathing through his mouth as he followed Tim into the next bedroom.

It had to have been a young girl's room, with the walls papered in a pattern of pink roses above high wooden baseboards. There was a small closet with an iron bar where metal hangers still clung, waiting to be used.

He stifled a sigh. How long had they waited, left by the girl who'd met a violent end?

A series of taps rapping on the window caused him to whip around. A dark branch, with clusters of broad, green leaves was pressed against the glass, swaying slightly in the breeze. When he stepped over to peer through, an ancient maple stood like a sentinel about thirty feet from the house, its branches like arms reaching over the expanse of lawn to the building.

"Normally, I'd say we should trim that tree but it makes an eerie sound tapping against the glass. It'll scare the crap out of whoever sleeps in this room." Tim's hands rose and his fingers fluttered, "Booga, booga!" punctuated with a wide grin and bobbing eyebrows.

"It's perfect." Brad walked out of the room smiling. It was a good thing that Gwen was still outside. He wouldn't blame her if she thought that their black sense of humour was sacrilegious or something.

The next room was about the same size, but the wallpaper was more suited for a young boy, with blue and green stripes. Crayon marks and stained plaster peeked out where the wallpaper had curled back. Brad stepped closer and he leaned over to decipher the red and purple marks.

Jonas? It had to be a very young boy because the 'J' and 'S' were backwards.

The hamburger he'd had for lunch before they left town, now felt like a lump of lead in his gut, and his hand rose to skitter across his stomach. The fact that it was a pre-schooler who'd slept in that room...had scrawled his name with crayons, only to meet a tragic end, was just plain wrong.

Tim had scurried on ahead of him and he shouted. "Holy shit. Look at this, Brad."

When he entered the last room on that side of the house, the sight of the blue lake outside caught his eye first. The room was a little larger than the first two bedrooms and the walls were painted a butter yellow shade. The cheerful colour and the lake outside made the room feel breezy, welcoming even.

"Seriously. If we didn't need the income from guests, I'd pick this room for myself. The one on the other side of this floor, is probably exactly the same." Tim turned and stared out at the lake, his fingers cupped lightly on the glass to shield his eyes from the glare of the sun casting diamonds on the water.

"I've got the feeling that this room was never used. Maybe a spare bedroom or guestroom?"

Brad walked across the wooden floor and nodded. Yes. That was one thing he'd have to agree with Tim on. The sense of sadness and foreboding he had felt in the other rooms was completely absent here.

The bedroom on the opposite side of the house mirrored the size and view of the lake, but it felt cold. It was still bright, with faded cream coloured paint, but a kidney-shaped dark blot marred the lighter colour of the wooden floor. For some reason, when Brad stepped into the room, he avoided stepping on the stain. The half digested burger rolled in his gut, but he couldn't tear his eyes away from the blotch on the floor. It looked like blood.

Even Tim seemed to be in more of a hurry to leave that room, flying by him to the other two bedrooms. It was clear that they had also been occupied by children, from the crayon graffiti and rips in the wallpaper.

Brad turned to follow Tim's thudding footsteps up the last set of stairs to the attic. There was no point in getting maudlin or sentimental about the former occupants of these rooms. What had happened, happened. What was done was done. This was an investment, nothing more. Instead of pondering about the past, he should be sizing the place up, looking for ways they could add to the atmosphere.

He walked across the last section of the hallway and climbed the stairs. Light from a window near the top of the stairs filtered over his face when he emerged. The roofline carved into the space, shortening the length of the rooms, but the dormer window popped out, revealing the lane and front lawn.

His eyes narrowed noticing the car parked below. Gwen stood there, her butt resting against her car, no longer on the phone but making no attempt to join them either. "Hmph." That confirmed her unease with being in the house—one more point in its favour.

He turned from the window to follow Tim's foot prints in the dust on the floor and cringed when he felt something brushing his cheek. With a sigh he raised his hand to clear the cobwebs away.

The floor was no longer dark hardwood but plain pine boards and the walls were a gray, stained plaster. It might have once been used for storage or even a playroom for the kids but now the bleak interior was home to spiders and mice.

Tim spun on his heels to face him, a smudge of dirt on the sleeve of his white shirt, while his hands brushed together quickly. "This will do for us, up here. You take the room on the other side and I can take this one." He looked around at the walls and sniffed, exhaling slowly. "It needs work—"

"Master of the understatement..." Brad wandered to the far end of the room and rubbed a spot on the window to see out. The lake seemed alive in the sparkling sunlight. Well, that was one positive thing. At least there was a window in a room that had all the charm and dimensions of a bowling alley.

"This will be control central. We'll install hidden cameras in the hallways and common areas downstairs and monitor everything from up here. That way, we'll know when we need a ghostly appearance, or a door to slam shut. And cold spots, that's a must as well. Direct the flow of air from an AC into areas that are spooky." Tim stood straight and put his hands in the back pockets of his jeans. "I think this is perfect for us."

Brad inhaled deeply and his cheeks billowed before exhaling slowly and nodding "It's a lot of work. We'll have three months to have it ready for October. I would expect *that* to be the best time to launch." He scratched his head and looked down at the floor. "Not a lot of time...?"

"That's *loads* of time. We're both due for vacation and *we* can do a lot of the work—well, the painting and cleaning. Maybe we can put in some trap doors and electronic gizmos—we'll probably have to hire that kind of stuff out, though. Plus my Dad will probably want to help. He's got plenty of time before ski season opens."

Brad's chest was light, leading the way out of the room. This was becoming more and more possible. They had enough money and they weren't afraid to work up a sweat. They could do this!

Behind him, Tim continued a running monologue. "If we're one of the few who've even bothered to come this far, to actually view the place, we have to low-ball the price. They're asking two, eighty-five? I say we try for two fifty...maybe even two forty. She said it's an estate sale. It's not like they've got money tied up in it or anything."

Brad nodded and continued to the other side. The door to what would be his room, was stuck and he had to shove his shoulder against it to get it to open. It let go suddenly and he almost fell into the room.

Oh my God! He jerked back and froze. There, in front of the blurry window was a ancient rocking chair. His breath caught in his throat, heart pounding hard. The rocking chair was moving, swaying back and forth!

Behind him Tim stopped in mid-sentence. Brad could feel his friend's breath, warm and moist on his neck. They both stared as the rocker continued to seesaw back and forth, neither of them daring to breathe.

Brad blinked repeatedly when the rocker's movement finally slowed, then stopped. He took a deep breath, while his mind scrambled for any sort of logical explanation. Keeping his eyes on the chair, he said quietly to Tim, "Did you see that?"

"Oh yeah."

"You think me shoving the door open caused that to happen?"

"Nope."

"What the hell is it doing up here anyway? Every single room in the house is empty!" Brad hissed.

"Beats me," Tim whispered back.

"And why is it set up right at the window? If you were sitting in it, you could watch the whole outside of this building!" Brad was barely moving his lips.

"Why are we whispering!" Tim said with a laugh. "Two things."

"Oh?"

"Yeah, first of all, that chair is really, really freaky."

"No kidding. What's number two?"

"I'm sure glad this is *your* room."

Brad turned and shoved at Tim's shoulder. "Tell you what. You take this room and I'll take the other. Even rationality has its limits. I'd never sleep a wink in here."

"Wimp." Tim grinned. "I've got the feeling that we'll be using that rocker again. It scared the shit out of you. Just wait till our guests see it rocking all on its own."

Chapter 6

Tim

"Brad? Tim? Yoo-hoo!"

At Gwen's high pitched yell, Tim jerked back, startled.

He gave his head a shake. The movement of the rocker could be explained by any number of reasons probably, but so what? The rocking chair just added another layer to the ambiance, totally eerie. *Exactly* what they wanted.

"We should go down. Gwen's waiting and we still have the basement and garage to check out. C'mon Brad." Tim turned and raced down the narrow set of stairs.

"We're on our way, Gwen," he hollered when they got down the attic stairs. When he reached the head of the second set of stairs Gwen's pinched face peered up at him. Her nerves and jumpiness were plain to see, in the way she held her hands tight together, the fingers rolling constantly over one another.

"Where's Brad? Is he okay?" Her gaze darted past him and she stepped forward.

"He's coming. Did you know they left an old rocking chair in the attic room?" His feet were a fast staccato, thudding on the stairs, but the smile on his face faded when he reached the bottom step.

Gwen's mouth gaped open and her eyes darted under a furrowed brow. "I don't remember seeing that when I listed the place. That's odd. My boss came with me to help with the measuring. I'll ask him if he remembers it."

39

At the sound of Brad's footsteps coming slowly down the steps, Tim turned and smiled. "No matter." He tried to read the expression on his friend's face. That whole episode with the chair really rattled Brad. Ha ha ha.

Tim put his hand on Gwen's shoulder and flashed another brilliant smile. "It was probably there but hey, it was a year ago, right? We'd better see the basement. Lead on Mac Duff."

Gwen managed a tight lipped smile that looked more like a grimace. She led the way down the hallway to the back of the house, bypassing the parlour and the library.

At a narrow, scarred door she stopped and turned the knob. Tim was right behind her. He hadn't noticed the door earlier, but then again, he'd been focussed on getting the back door open. Her hand rose and the dark opening became lit with a yellowish glow when she hit the light switch at the top of the steps.

His lips stiffened into a scowl. As bad as the cobwebs were in the attic, it was nothing to the silken sheets fluttering in the basement stairwell. He hated cobwebs; they were gross and the idea of them getting in his hair... with spider eggs... it was disgusting.

Gwen plucked an envelope from her purse and began sweeping her hand forward, clearing a path as she stepped gingerly down the steps. Following her down, the air was cool, but it was also sour in his nostrils, with an aroma of decay. When his foot landed at the bottom, he looked down at the packed dirt floor. Yuck. It was slimy and damp.

He glanced over his shoulder, glad to see Brad following him down. The really creepy thing about this house was the basement. Who knew what bugs and vermin infested the place? His arms crossed over his chest and his fingers scratched absently. Ghosts, goblins and spooks were imaginary. Spiders, mice and centipedes were *real*.

Gwen was halfway across the large empty space, shining a small penlight on a dusty, metal panel. "This is the electrical service. It had been updated to accommodate modern appliances." She pointed to a heavy-duty, wall plug and boards neatly lined up on the dirt floor under it. "This is where the laundry is."

"*No fucking way!*" The words popped out before Tim could censor them. He glanced at Gwen and muttered, "Sorry." But there was no way he'd ever come down to this dungeon to wash his clothes. He felt dirty just being down there, breathing the damp, mouldy air.

His brain kick started to a new thought and he looked at Gwen. "It's going to cost a lot to change this and set the laundry in the kitchen."

"Yes, well...all of the improvements you need to do will be reflected in what you offer. That is, if you still want to buy it. There are two other houses to look at today. One of them may be a better fit for you guys." She followed Brad over to where he stood staring at a huge metal object. A monstrous box, it had large tin pipes sticking out all over it, snaking throughout the basement ceiling.

Seeing his quizzical look, she said, "The furnace is old, but it works. We call these octopuses. They're ancient but reliable even if they're not the most energy efficient."

Tim's sigh underscored the fact that he'd just brought the offering price down to two hundred thirty, in his mind. Actually, before they got that far, they would have to get an inspection and ballpark on the cost of replacing this beast.

Brad drifted away to another dark hulking object tucked tight to the wall across from the furnace. It was covered with a rotten, old piece of cloth that he gingerly lifted up. A musical note reverberated in the room. "What's a piano doing down *here*?"

Gwen blew a sigh through puffed cheeks. "Who knows? Can you imagine trying to get it up those stairs? If you don't want it, we can ask the owners to break it down and remove it."

Tim smiled to himself. It actually added to the creep factor in the house. A bonus if they bought it.

There was lots of work to be done in the house, but after the washer and dryer were set up on the main level the worst would be over. This place was the one. He felt it in his bones.

He jumped and his squeak was girlish when a mouse poked its nose out of a hole in the wall next to his head.

Add fumigator to the list.

He hurried back up the stairs, ignoring Brad's taunt and mimic of his squeal. His shoulders shuddered and he exhaled loudly. Fine by him. Let Brad be the one to go down there to change fuses and check on the furnace.

Taking the lead again, Gwen led them outside. Across the driveway was a wooden building with a broad metal door at the front. Tim's jaw tightened as he took in the building from the gray metal roof to the dark wooden walls. He wasn't sure if he'd ever want to park his car in that place. It might fall down any minute.

This time he let Brad follow Gwen, while he took up the rear position going through the heavy wooden door. He got a slight whiff of engine oil and grease, but his eyebrows rose seeing how clean and tidy the large room was. Heavy, wooden, beams crossed in struts that supported the roof like a cathedral. Near the back of the building, a ladder was perched against a platform above the main room.

He nodded and walked over to it, testing his foot on the first rung. It was solid enough. He climbed up and peeked into the dark space. A few boxes and tools were scattered as well as the rounded arch of the hull of a cedar canoe. Great. They could use that, being on the lake. And, they'd need a place for the lawn mower and tools. This place would do for that.

He climbed back down and brushed his shirt and pants off. "So that's the buildings. Let's see the land and the shore. "

When they emerged once more into the bright, summer day, he shielded his eyes, staring to the end of the property. The property line was defined by a low, wooden fence, that ran along in a straight line, overgrown with wild grapevine in places.

Gwen took the spot between them, walking slowly over the lawn, now turned to a field with tall grass and bright yellow and blue wild flowers poking through. At the left side of the property a row of stately trees and bushes edged the opposite side like a bookend.

Gwen pointed to the trees and turned to flash a smile at each of them. "There's a pretty stream over there that flows down to the lake. When I first saw it, I thought what a cool spot to sit and read a book."

Tim looked over to where she pointed. What the...? His eyebrows drew together, and he squinted trying to see. There had been something there. There it was again! He was able to make out a slight whisper of white flitting behind the lush green foliage. He blinked and it was gone; there were only the trees and bushes now.

He looked over at Brad but there was no sign his friend had seen it. Brad just looked ahead as he walked beside Gwen. Sure, it probably was just some trick of the sunlight and a breeze moving the leaves. Of course that had to be it. But hopefully it had been more. It *was* more; he knew what he saw. But if he was wrong, they'd create the effect. It was a good one.

They continued on and stepped into the copse of trees, the only sound breaking the stillness of the air was the gurgle and splash of water, cascading over stones.

Tim glanced around, searching for any sign of white, a piece of fabric or paper that had been swept along from the main road and onto the property. But there was only the shaded spots the green leaves cast, highlighted in the dappled sunlight.

The stream wound gently down to the lake, the clear water following the groove created by years of spring run-off, rain and, of course, the underground spring miles away. It was peaceful and beautiful, especially when the blue vista of the lake opened up.

Tim walked along the shore line and his shoulders rolled forward for a moment. A shiver scuttled up his spine and he turned his head to peer at the attic room.

They were being watched. Right now. From the attic!

He smiled. Maybe it was silly nonsense thinking that someone was watching him. But if *he* felt this way—they were *really* onto a winner.

Chapter 7

Brad
A week later...

Brad raised his glass and clinked it against Tim's. "To us and our success with the Haunted Inn." He took a long sip of champagne, feeling the bubbles tickle his nostrils.

Across the table, Tim emptied the glass and set it down with a bang. He grinned, shaking his head from side to side, staring at the set of papers in front of him. He picked up the accepted offer Gwen had dropped off and said, "I still can hardly believe it. We picked it up for a song. We practically stole it. It was too easy for words."

"Hey!" Brad grabbed the bottle of champagne and topped their glasses up. "Not all that easy. Remember the first guy who'd done the inspection—McGready. I thought he'd have a heart attack when he went into that front bedroom."

Tim let out a guffaw of laughter, slapping the table with his palm. "Oh my God, yes! After he made the sign of the cross, he almost broke his neck flying down the stairs to get the hell out of there."

Brad sat back picturing the retired builder, his watery blue eyes darting everywhere, looking over his shoulder constantly. "But at least he tried. Not like the first guy we called." Brad looked up at the ceiling. "What was his name?"

"Alder. Alan Alder."

Brad snapped his fingers. "Yeah, that's right! *That* guy was weird. He was all interested at first, then when I told him the address, he said 'No way, Jose,' and hung up!"

Tim sat back in his chair. "Ka—ching" Rubbing his fingers across his thumb. "The place has got a rep already. Thank God we found that Comstock guy. He was a bit steep in price but pretty thorough...and not easily spooked."

Brad was silent for a few moments, his fingers toying with the rim of his glass. "I told Sophie about the house when I saw her yesterday. Not about the history—the murder suicide— just that we found a place that will work for us." He looked up at Tim. "She wants to see it."

Tim sighed. When he answered, his face was tight. "Not yet. Promise me, you'll wait until we've signed all the papers next week, and actually own the place." He took another long swallow of the champagne and let out a small burp. "Look Brad, I know you really like her, but you've only been going out with her for a few months." He took a deep breath and blew it slowly from puffed cheeks. "Hey, you probably think I'm biased because I think she's a little weird. Maybe I am. But I'm also your best friend. This project could make us set for life. It's too important to us to risk any second thoughts on your part."

Brad sadly shook his head as he stared across the table at his friend. Tim just didn't like Sophie, that was all there was to it. They were like oil and water together and there were times when he felt like he walked a tight rope between them.

If Tim knew how strongly she'd come out against him being involved in the supernatural, Tim would be pissed. On the other hand, if Sophie had any inkling of the ghastly history of the house, she'd have a conniption fit.

Brad smiled and shook his head. "I won't get cold feet. The money we stand to make with this...that's my number one concern."

He met Tim's sceptical glare, head on. "You think I'm whipped, don't you?" He snorted and picked up his glass, holding it before him. "You'll see. Sure, I really like her, but this is my life. If she's ever going to be more than just a girlfriend, there are some things she'll have to accept."

"Yeah right." Tim laughed. "You're trying to sound like me and there can only be one of me. They broke the mold."

"Thank God." Brad rolled his eyes, but Tim continued on.

"After we close the deal. Bring her out as often as you want. Hell, give her a mop and bucket and tell her to go to town with it, cleaning. But she doesn't get to see it before we own the joint. She'd hate the place, get all 'spooky sensitive' and shit and probably try to talk you out of it."

Brad's arms crossed over his chest and he took a deep breath. It was no use talking to Tim about this. Definitely not worth any kind of falling out, not on the cusp of a big business venture. He forced a smile and looked over at his friend. "When's your Dad coming to see it?"

The hypocrisy of the situation annoyed Brad, seeing the smile flash on Tim's face. Tim's Dad was okay to see it but Sophie wasn't?

"Wednesday. Gwen is lending me the key so she doesn't have to come. He's staying overnight at a B&B. Mom wanted to come but there're a few guests in the hotel, so she can't." Tim's fingers thrummed on the table top and he looked across at Brad. "What about your Dad? Aren't you going to ask him to have a look at it?"

"Ask my Dad? I'm not sure where he is right now. Last I heard he was in Spain." His finger circled the rim of the glass again. He grimaced, thinking about his father. Since the divorce, he hardly ever saw his parents, both of them busy with their new freedom, dating and going on cruises. The only one who would take an interest was Jody, his younger sister, but she was at school in another city. The breaches in his own family life hit hard sometimes. He hadn't even told any of them yet about this venture.

Which made him appreciate what he had with Tim and Sophie even more.

Tim was the brother he'd never had, even if they'd only know each other for five years. After a rocky beginning, forced to share a room in first year university, tolerance had blossomed into a lasting friendship.

Brad looked down into his glass of wine, picturing Sophie. He'd liked her right from the start. From the captivating green eyes, the crazy second hand chic of her clothing to her appreciation of the absurd in life. Sure, she had her quirks, who didn't? But the times he'd spent with her, walking along the waterfront, dancing and just quietly holding each other watching an old corny movie...well, she was special.

Tim stood up and finished the last of his wine. "Y'know Brad, you're welcome to come with us. I mean, when Dad and I go out to the house."

Tim's Dad was nice and all that but something this big was a moment to be shared only by family—the first major investment a son made, that a father could proudly acknowledge.

He wasn't jealous of Tim...not really. He just wished that things had turned out differently with his own Mom and

Dad. Maybe then, he'd have family to fall back on like Tim had.

"Thanks, but I'll take a pass."

"At least have dinner with us after. Dad would be disappointed if he didn't see you at all when he's in town." Tim set the glass on the counter and turned to face him. "What do you say?"

"Absolutely. I'd like that. What are you doing tonight?" Enough of the conversation about Tim's Dad.

Tim grinned and his eyebrows bobbed up and down. "You need to ask? I got a date. Remember that waitress last week?" He fished in his pocket and drew the piece of paper out, scanning it with his eyes.

Brad shook his head and sighed. "Carly?" Shit. Tim didn't even remember her name? He had to look at the paper? "Just remember you have work tomorrow. And so do I!" Brad wandered over to the living room and flopped down on the sofa.

"Don't worry. It's a first date. We're going to that *Haunted* movie. What do you think of that?"

"Oh! The one we walked out on *after* buying the tickets? That one?"

"We walked out of *Star Wars,* buddy," Tim bantered back. "And into bigger and better things," he said, gesturing at the documents on the table.

Brad put his hands behind his head and stretched out his legs. "Still want to see it." He pointed a finger at Tim. "And you're buying the next time, pal."

Tim fished his cell phone from his pocket and keyed in her number. "Yeah, whatever." Before pressing 'call', he said, "I wonder if I'll be able to write off this date? Seeing the movie could be construed as research, you know."

"Great. Becoming a multi-tasker now? Research and romance?" Brad grinned and settled higher, propping his back against the arm rest.

Tim grinned. "I'm just going to focus on the romance now," he said and pressed 'call'.

Brad shook his head and pulled his own phone out of his pocket. He'd send some texts to his family and let them know about his venture and get it over with. With Tim out of the house, he'd call Sophie, maybe see if she wanted to go out for coffee or an ice cream. With any luck she'd just invite him over for the night.

Chapter 8

Tim

Tim grinned watching his father wander through the rooms in the main floor of the house. He could tell from the look on the old man's face that he approved. Even so, it was good to hear it as well.

"So? What do you think?"

His father stopped and turned his gaze from the plaster ceiling to Tim's face. His eyes crinkled in the corners and the lines bordering his mouth deepened. "It's a sound building. I think you did all right, kid."

It was the best kind of praise that John Holland ever gave to any of his kids. Even when Tim's brother, Robert had won the downhill slalom ski competition in the junior class division, the best he'd got was 'ya did okay, kid.' Maybe it was his British background that made him a master of understatement.

His chest expanded, feeling a lightness that was at odds with the heavy atmosphere of the house. It was a moment between a father and son, some kind of rite of passage that he'd passed with flying colours. Tim rocked back and forth from heel to toe, his hands deep in his pocket, affecting an air of nonchalance that he sure didn't feel.

"Yeah, and the price...we got it for fifty one thousand under list price. I think we did pretty well."

John moved over to his son and clapped him on the back. "I have to admit, if anyone actually believes in ghosts and haunted houses, this place sure fits the bill. Too bad your mother couldn't make it today. She believes in this paranormal stuff. She claims she saw her grandmother the day after the woman died."

Tim's head jerked back. "She never told me that."

John laughed. "Well it happened a long time ago, when she was a teenager." He nodded his head and looked around once more. "I think you're going to make some money off this project."

"I've done some digging on the internet. There are some places in the States that specialize in a haunted night experience, but there's nothing around here. I think we're getting in on the ground floor with this." Tim nodded his head to the side, and led the way up the heavy oak staircase.

"Glad to see you putting that college education to good use." John cast a smug smile over at his son. "Maybe I'll look into places in Tremblant. There's a vacant place that's been for sale forever that I pass when I go jogging. It's a huge house, kind of like this one."

"Oh yeah? Out the old sawmill road? You still run there, right? I think I remember the place." Tim's eyes narrowed. Some friends of his in grade school had asked him to join them there one Halloween night, just run down the driveway and knock on the door. It had seemed kind of pointless to him, especially when there was so much loot and candy to be had in the village.

"Yeah. I like the forest and the quiet when I run. There's only a couple houses there and hardly any traffic. Your mother's not fussy about me running in such a remote spot but, what the hey? You only live once, right? Why not do the things you like?"

Tim grinned and opened the first door on the second floor. "Exactly. And running a haunted house as opposed to being a corporate shill appeals to me. More money in my pocket for the work I do, right?"

John stepped into the bathroom and his eyes took everything in. He turned to look at his son and his face was serious. "So, the story...a family was *actually* murdered here, right?" When Tim nodded, he continued. "Can you believe that? Then that'll be a selling point in your marketing. Gruesome I know, but it'd be effective."

Tim walked down the hall to the first bedroom, the one that looked like a little boy's room. "For sure. We're going to get—"

A deafening 'BANG!' from the downstairs made them both freeze. Tim looked over at his Dad to see the man's eyes as big as his own.

"What the hell?" His father's words were whispered before he turned and looked over the railing to the floor below. "Did we leave the door open or something?"

Tim's heart was a racehorse in his chest and his knees had turned to jelly. "No. I made sure I closed it." He joined his father at the railing. "Sometimes Dad, I believe this place could really be haunted."

His father snorted but his face was blanched of colour when he turned to face Tim. "Yeah. Right." He cupped his hands over his mouth and leaned over the railing. "BOOO to you, buddy!" he called. Turning back to Tim he said, "C'mon. Let's finish up here and then we'll check downstairs to see what fell over."

Tim nodded and took a deep breath to get his heart and body to slow down again. His father was right. The noise had been startling, that was all. In the empty house, any noise would be amplified to the extreme.

He followed his father back into the child's bedroom, watched him step over to the window and look out over the expanse of lawn.

"So you and Brad...you've kept a reserve of money for renovations and repairs? I've always found that whatever you estimate in time or money, double it and you'll end up closer to the real cost. If you need money, we've got plenty to help you out. Consider it an advance on your inheritance."

Tim looked down at the floor for a moment. Even though eventually his parents would die, it wasn't something he liked to think about. His parents were only in their mid fifties, and they were both healthy as horses. They'd be around for many, many years to come with any luck.

He put his hand on his Dad's arm. "Hey Dad, don't say stuff like that, okay? It gives me the creeps." He looked over at his father's weathered face, the edge of grey hair at is temple and shook his head. "If we do need money, I'll consider it a loan and pay you back."

John looked at his son and smiled. "How about Brad? His parents see the place yet? What do they think?"

Tim sighed and stepped out of the room to continue the tour. "No. And they're not likely to." He paused and turned to look at his father. "Do me a favour? Please don't ask about them at dinner tonight. Since his parents split, Brad's family's not close with each other at all, and sometimes, I think he envies what I have."

John once more clapped his son on the back and nodded. "Absolutely. The poor kid."

There were times when Tim envied the money Brad's family had. But overall, he wouldn't trade what he had with his own family with what Brad had to deal with.

When they stepped off the last step and into the foyer, Tim and his father exchanged a look. The door was closed, which could have accounted for the bang but Tim didn't think that was it. He led the way to the parlour and then to the dining room. Everything was in order. actually the only thing that could have made the loud noise was if a shelf fell, but they were still intact.

A walk through to the kitchen and greenhouse, also turned up blank.

Tim turned to his father, "See? Who knows what made that noise?"

His father shrugged his shoulders and looked up at the ceiling. "I don't know. But y'know something? Things that go bang in the afternoon are scarier than things that go bump in the night, huh?" He turned and let Tim lead the way out of the house, to check out the waterfront.

Neither one saw the crack that ran the length of the basement door.

Chapter 9

Brad

The back of Sophie's pint sized Honda Civic was packed with cleaning supplies while Brad's knees dented the dashboard of the car. Warm summer air rushed into the open windows, the old car's only recourse in the battle with the heat of the day.

With auburn hair swirling over her cheeks, she turned and flashed a smile; her sparkling eyes narrow with laughter. Brad fell into her gaze, resisting the urge to tuck the locks of her hair behind her ears. She was a pretty wood nymph, a playful sprite decked out in a loud paisley skirt and yellow tank top, her nails sporting a hot pink.

"Actually, I'm dying to see it. I'm still not sure I like the premise of the venture, hoodwinking guests but, Caveat Emptor, I suppose." She took a long sip of the take-out coffee and turned once more to the road.

He looked away quickly, his gaze on the fields and trees skimming by. If she knew the truth, that the house really did have a gruesome history, she'd like it even less. But there was no way he'd ever tell her about it.

He turned to her once more, "It's nice of you to offer help with the cleaning. God knows, it needs it."

"Glad to help." She glanced over at him. "I'm just sorry I have to bail before dinner. You're sure Tim will be able to give you a lift back to town? He's bringing his latest girlfriend, isn't he?" She did an exaggerated roll of her eyes and heaved a sigh.

Brad cleared his throat and looked down at his lap for a moment. Sophie was as much a fan of Tim's freewheeling sex life as he was. "Yes, Carly. She's nice. I met her a couple times at the apartment. She's a bit of a gypsy, travelling across the country, only staying in one place long enough to finance the next leg of her journey. Tim might have met his match with this one. She's as much a free spirit as he is." He chuckled. "And for a change, I think he really likes her."

Sophie grinned and tapped his knee. "What? More than just the sex? I like her already. It's time someone showed him what's it's like to be on the receiving end of that schtick." She looked serious for a moment, her full lips frowning. "I bet he's a nice guy underneath all that . If he'd only let himself show it."

Brad took a deep breath, deciding to let it go. She wasn't nearly as hard on Tim as he was on her, making fun of her New Age mysticism. It was one of the reasons that when they spent the night together, it was usually at her apartment.

The turn to the property was just ahead and he pointed to it. "There. On the left." His stomach was filled with butterflies and he leaned forward, easing the pressure on his knees. Everything was working out as planned, so far. He really hoped Sophie and Tim would get along today.

Tim's Dad had liked the place so much that he wanted to come in on the venture as an investor. He said he might start looking at other places up in the Laurentians that were like their house.

Their house. He took a deep breath and grinned.

Even at work, things were looking up. They'd had no problem scheduling their vacation, to work on the place. It was wonderful. Two weeks without going into the penitentiary, scheduling tests, filing and inputting data. Honestly, it was soooo boring.

Sophie flipped the turn signal on and the car slowed to make the turn. When the blue vista opened up before them, her mouth fell open. "Oh my God. Look at that." She reached over and lightly punched Brad's arm. "You're so lucky! Seriously, I know where I'm gonna spend some time this summer. I'd like to go canoeing on the lake."

Once more he was struck with the imposing stone structure of the building, the high windows and warp around veranda. It really was an awesome place. The attached greenhouse and outbuildings and the murmuring brook that fed to the lake. It was like being Lord of the Manor.

Tim's SUV was parked out front but there was no sign of him or Carly. They were probably hard at it already. And by hard at it, it had better be cleaning! There was too much to do for screwing around.

The car stopped next to Tim's and he turned to smile at Sophie, about to say, 'we're here' but the look on her face stopped him cold.

Her eyes were so wide, they appeared to be close to popping out onto her cheeks and her hand covered her mouth.

"You're blown away aren't you?" His breath hitched in his chest, peering over at her, hoping against hope that she'd agree. But there was no mistaking the shadow of fear that had settled in her stiff body and gaping eyes. "What's wrong?"

"Brad. Tell me, you haven't bought this place." Her voice was soft, barely above a whisper. She gripped the steering wheel with ivory knuckles, leaning forward, taking in all of the building, but lingering on the top floor.

His jaw muscle clenched and he turned to her. "Sophie! What the heck is wrong with you? Of course we bought it! You know that."

Suddenly the car felt claustrophobic, his knees hurting where the dashboard dug in. He opened the car door and got out, turning his head to see her join him. But she sat still as a stone, sheltered behind the steering wheel.

The vein in his temple pulsed and his hands balled into tight fists as he strode around the car and opened her door. "Come on. I know it looks a bit imposing but it's—"

"Gruesome." Her lips snapped shut and she took a long breath through flared nostrils, her fingers still clinging to the steering wheel.

"Gruesome? Come on! That's harsh. It needs some TLC, a little elbow grease, but you'll see. It's okay." He reached for her, holding his hand out to help her from the low slung car.

She turned and stared at him silently for a few moments, seeming to come to some sort of decision. "I'm only doing this for you. If it were up to me, I'd never set foot on this ground." She undid her seat belt and then swallowed hard, looking up at him.

"It's okay, Sophie. You'll see." He felt like a kid coaxing a kitten down from a tree. What was wrong with her? Sure, the house was creepy, but really? Not so creepy that you wouldn't even get out of the car!

Her hand was damp and tiny in his, and he smiled to reassure her. When her foot touched the ground, she swallowed hard, and seemed to stifle a gag. The smile faded from his face as he peered at her.

She stood before him and her eyes closed slowly, breathing deeply. Whatever was going on with her, was affecting her in a real *physical* way. "The air," she said, "it's thick... the air's like pea soup, closing in on me." Her hand went to her neck and she opened her eyes to look at Brad, wild eyed.

He stepped closer and put his arm around her waist, giving her some support. "Just breathe, Sophie. Relax and breathe. You're having some sort of panic attack or something." But his heart thudded hard in his chest watching her. He'd never forgive himself if this was actually hurting her.

For a few minutes, she did just that, breathing deeply while her lips moved in some sort of silent chant. When she opened her eyes, the vivid green was a sharp contrast to the paleness of her cheeks.

"Would you like a glass of water?" His other hand rose to cup her cheek. Her skin was hot and dry and he swore he felt her body tremble despite the warmth of the day. If he'd thought she was feigning this or even just over-reacting he didn't now.

"No. No water."

"Come over to the veranda and sit on the step for a moment. Maybe the heat is getting to you. It's over eighty in the shade. That *has* to be it." He led her slowly across the driveway and held her hands firmly in his while she lowered to sit on the wide, wooden step.

Her eyes closed once more and a tear trickled down her cheek. "So much sadness and rage here." She pulled her hands from his and cupped her face with them. "Oh God...those poor children. Their screams and absolute terror." Her voice was muffled behind her hands. Her shoulders began to heave.

Brad's blood went cold hearing her words. How could she have known? He'd had the odd, niggling thought of those kids every time he was in the house, but Sophie? Her response was off the charts and she hadn't even set foot in the place yet!

When the door opened, Tim and Carly spilled out onto the veranda, the laughter they'd shared doused like the flame of a candle, gaping at Sophie.

Tim stepped forward and placed his hand on her shoulder. His eyes bored into Brad's. "What's going on? Are you okay, Sophie?"

"I'll get her some pop. There's a cold one in the cooler." Carly backed away, her hand on her chest, going back into the house.

Sophie's hands lowered and her eyes were red rimmed, looking first at Tim and then back to Brad. "You can't stay here. This was a horrible mistake buying this place." She pointed at the front door. "A *whole family* was slaughtered here! This place is evil!"

Brad's chest was tight and his heart raced in his chest at her words. His fingers laced through his hair and he stared at the ground for a few moments.

Tim stepped back and his arms crossed over his chest. "What the hell? It wasn't a mistake. This place is going to be great! We certainly *are* staying here." He thrust a finger at her. "You'll see! People will pay big money to stay here too." He glanced over at Brad and did a huge roll of his eyes. "You told her, didn't you?"

Brad's mouth was suddenly dry. He shook his head slowly from side to side. "I didn't tell her a thing, man." Somehow, she'd picked up on something and she *knew*. She'd told him that she *sensed* things.

61

A scream pierced the stillness behind them, coming from inside the house.

Brad's heart jumped into his throat and Tim spun around, but before he could reach for the handle of the door, it opened and Carly was framed in the dark woodwork. Her eyes were wide and in her hand was a can of pop, bubbling over the lid and onto her fingers.

"It was a mouse. I freaking *hate* mice." Her cheeks became pink and she looked down at the floor, stomping her foot for emphasis.

Sophie stepped away from the step and turned to face them. She made the sign of the cross over her forehead and shoulders, her mouth a straight gash in her face. "It was more than that. Your house is possessed."

"No, Sophie. C'mon. I'll walk down to the lake with you. We'll sit on the dock and dangle our feet in the water. "Brad stepped towards her and folded her in his arms, patting her back gently.

He could feel her silent sobs in the racking of her shoulders. Oh God. This was a nightmare. Little by little he eased back and then kissed her forehead. With his thumbs he wiped the tears from her eyes and led her down the path to the water.

She clung to him, walking silently beside him. "Brad, there's an evil presence here that you can't mess with. Murder and death live on in that house. I saw something in the top window staring down at me. It wants you gone or it will kill you." She glanced over her shoulder at the house again before stepping onto the dock. "It's still there, watching."

Brad's skin felt like a million ants were scraping over him. He knew what she meant. How many times had he felt the same thing, that someone or something was watching him? But even if it was a left-over energy of that last family, the tragic horror, it couldn't actually hurt them. Creep them out, sure. But actually kill them? That was preposterous. Who ever heard of a ghost killing you?

As they lowered themselves down onto the rough worn slats of the dock, she glanced over at him. "The money is not worth your life, Brad. Leave. Come back to town with me. I don't expect Tim to believe it but you? Surely you trust me on this."

He put his arm around her and pulled her close."Sophie, I can't." His gut felt like someone had given him a good punch. This was it. The moment of truth. "It's not that I don't think you're sincere in what you believe, but I just don't think this place is as dangerous as you seem to think."

She pulled back and her eyes were narrow slits staring at him. "Oh yeah? Then why did I sense such terror and pain? *People died there*! I know it! I sense these things, like a dog can smell footsteps on a trail or hear sounds we can't. Don't you see that?"

He held his hands up in partial surrender to her point. "Okay! Say, I agree that you feel or sense things? That doesn't mean I feel threatened physically in the house. A ghost, if that's what it is, can't physically hurt me. It's smoke and mirrors. I'm flesh; I'm alive."

She huffed a sarcastic sigh. "You think you're all macho, all rational and immune. It doesn't work like that." She turned slightly and the next thing he knew she was standing, looking down at him. "I can't stay here and watch this happen to you. Even to Tim. The longer I sit here, the sicker I feel."

He went to stand up but her hand on his shoulder stopped him. "Don't bother. There's nothing more I can say. Good bye."

He watched her leave, striding by Tim and Carly who had wandered down the path to join them. After she passed by them, she broke into a sprint, jumping into her car and throwing gravel and dust up from the wheels of her car as she gunned it up the driveway.

Well, that was that. There was no doubt in his mind, nor in his heart they were through. He closed his eyes, willing the tears back, and took a deep breath.

Chapter 10

Tim

"Possessed!" Tim voice was low watching Sophie stride by and get in her car. His arm went around Carly's shoulder and he pulled her close. "*She's* possessed!" He grabbed the can of pop from Carly's hand and downed half of it in a few swallows.

Brad joined them watching the plume of dust rise behind Sophie's car.

"That was kind of strange." Carly looked from Brad to Tim. "What is she? Some kind of a witch or something?"

Tim's risked a peek at Brad. The poor guy...but what the hell did he expect? It was just so typical of Sophie, to be so theatrical about seeing the place. She had to go and try to spoil everything, didn't she? "She's *says* she's a witch, or sensitive or whatever bullshit term they're using. To me, she's just a damn drama queen."

Brad ambled over to the step. His hand rubbed the back of his neck and his smile was sheepish when he turned to face them. "Well, that's that. You were right about what she'd think."

Big surprise there. Tim's jaw muscle ached, he was clenching it so hard. "Maybe her reaction is a good thing. If *she* gets that freaked out, we know we got something. " He looked down at Carly and kissed the top of her head. "How 'bout you? Any bad vibes in this place?"

Her chin rose and she smiled up at him. "Just the bloody mouse, so far." She turned to gaze up the driveway where the dust was just now dissipating. "Too bad. We could have used her help."

Brad turned and gave Tim a funny look. "Nice to see Carly's part of the 'us'—helping out and all." His shoulders were slumped when he stepped into the house, carrying the weight of the world.

Oh shit. Tim's sighed. It wasn't like Carly was trying to horn in. And now was not the time for any lecture on his retinue of girlfriends.

She pressed her hip into his, turning them both around and gave his butt a swat. "Come on slacker. Those rooms won't clean themselves."

He laughed and grabbed for her waist, trying to tickle her above the waistband of her shorts. When she squealed and raced ahead, her ebony pony tail swaying from side to side, he couldn't help compare her to Sophie. Carly was full of life, always smiling and laughing, whereas Sophie was just too weird. A body could only stand so much seriousness and drama.

When he entered the kitchen, Brad turned to face him. "What the fuck?"

Holy shit! Every door of the oak kitchen cabinets was open and the drawers were extended out to their fullest length. But not only that, water hissed loudly from the kitchen faucet. Tim's legs were suddenly weak.

"The same thing in the powder room! The cabinet doors are all open and the water's running full blast!" Carly's voice called from the hallway.

"It was like this when I came in. We were all outside..." Brad's eyes were wide and his mouth fell open. "Sophie? Was this because she was—"

"I don't know what's going on here." Tim strode forward and turned the tap off. He shoved the drawers closed and shut the cabinets with a bang. "And I don't care!"

Looking at the dazed look on Brad's face, he felt a surge of anger rush through his muscles. "Snap out of it and check the upstairs. Start with the bathroom."

Brad gave his head a shake. "Yeah," he said and went upstairs.

Tim turned and leaned against the counter, his eyebrows tight while he stared at the floor trying to gather his thoughts. This was totally off the wall. He took a few deep breaths and looked up to see Carly wander into the kitchen, a puzzled look on her face.

"Tim? This place is weird." She slipped her hands in the back pockets of her jean shorts, standing in front of him.

"Yeah, that's part of the charm, right? But we can't let this hold us up. As you said, we've got work to do." His hand rose to rub the back of his neck and he chuckled. "If we could only control whatever energy opened the cabinets and turned on the water...it's exactly what we want when guests are here."

Brad's footsteps thudded on the stairs and then he showed up in the kitchen, a perplexed look on his face. "The sink and the tub faucets were on full blast as well. Whatever's in this house, it sure has a thing for water."

Tim decided this wasn't getting them anywhere, standing around speculating on what had happened. He pushed away from the counter. "Who knows?"

At the sound of water running full force in the kitchen sink, he turned to watch Carly, standing there, filling a bucket. "Don't worry. It's *me* this time." She laughed and shooed him away. "I'll do the kitchen and these drawers better not fly open or assault me, or I'll sue you guys."

"Good luck with that one. After buying this place we're tapped out." Tim picked up a broom and dustpan to head out to the greenhouse to begin cleaning there. From the corner of his eye he noticed Brad drag the vacuum across the floor and disappear into the hallway.

He stepped into the greenhouse and his head jerked back, staring with wide eyes. "What the..." There was an open book laying on the shelf next to the old pottery. He flipped the cover to see what it was. The *Alchemist* book. The last time he's seen the book was three weeks ago and he'd put it back in the box.

Taking a deep breath, he shook his head a little. This was just more of the same. He clapped the book shut and set it back in the box under the table.

***

It was mid-afternoon by the time they decided to break for lunch. They carried their food down to the dock, dangling their feet in the water while they ate.

Carly looked over and grinned. "You know...sitting out here in the sun, it's hard to believe the stuff that happened." She kicked her feet splashing droplets of water. "If I go back in there and things are messed up or something weird is going on in that kitchen I cleaned, I'm gonna be pissed." She chuckled and then the smile dropped from her lips. "Seriously...that was spooky."

Tim looked over at Brad. "Shit. We should have taken pictures of it. I'm sure that would have come in handy at some point...maybe in marketing."

"Yeah, probably. We'll know for next time." Brad's voice was soft and he looked distracted.

He was still hurting from that blow-up with Sophie. Why the hell should a guy let a girl get under his skin so easily? There were plenty of fish in the sea after all.

As if Carly sensed it as well, she grinned and kicked once more in the water. "Wish I'd brought my bathing suit. After slaving in that kitchen, the water sure is tempting."

Tim polished off his soda. "There's no one around, other than Brad. He and I will be going up soon. Peel off and skinny dip, if you want."

Brad got to his feet and looked down, smiling at Carly. "Help yourself. I'd say you earned it. The kitchen's so clean you could eat off the floor." His footsteps reverberated on the stillness of the water as he trudged across the wooden platform.

She smiled and winked her eye, looking at him. "Come with me." In a flash, the tank top was up and over her head.

He looked away, but not before he'd caught a glimpse of the lacy white bra and the swell of her breast. It was so tempting to give in. But there'd be plenty of time for fooling around with Carly after they'd put in a full day's work.

"Maybe later. Don't swim out too far." He stood up and strode off the dock, waving his hand over his shoulder at her. There was no way he'd risk another look as she peeled the rest of her clothes off. A guy could only take so much.

He smiled hearing the splash of water and her shriek at the cold temperature. His hand was on the railing of the veranda when a blood curdling scream pierced the stillness of the day.

Spinning around, his heart was in his throat. He scanned the water near the dock for some sign of her. His feet flew on the flagstone path. The only indication that she was in there were the bubbles that roiled to the surface.

"CARLY?"

Brad was right behind him, his footsteps pounding. "What happened? Where's Carly?"

When his foot touched the first plank of the dock, she bobbed to the surface, a web of dark hair streaming over her cheeks. Her arms were like windmills, pulling through the water to reach the dock.

"Are you all right? What happened?" He knelt and extended his hand to pull her closer.

She was white as a sheet, her eyes wide with terror as she grasped his hand. "Something grabbed my ankle! It tugged me under!" Naked, she was actually climbing his arm to get back on the dock, way past caring that Brad was also there.

As she struggled to get out of the water she began to scream.

"It still has me! Get it off! Get it off of meeee!"

With one final heave, Tim pulled Carly out of the water and onto the dock. She lay on her back, kicking her legs. "Get it off! Get it off!"

Wrapped around her foot was a sodden, filthy piece of fabric. Tim grabbed it and yanked it from her limb, tossing it aside onto the deck. He tore his t-shirt off and in a flash covered her up.

She was terror stricken, her eyes huge. "Wha—what is it?" she said, goggling at the sodden heap on the deck of the pier.

Brad bent over and picked it up. Holding it by its edge, he shook it out.

Although it was torn and smudged with algae and mud, it was plainly a young girl's dress. Old fashioned, trimmed with now ragged lace, it reminded Tim him of photos he'd seen of little girls in first communion dresses. What the hell was a little girl's dress doing in the lake?

"Eeew! Throw it away!" Carly tugged the hem of Tim's shirt down and scrabbled away on the deck, disgust oozing from her pores. "That fucking thing almost drowned me!"

Tim signalled with a nod and a look for Brad to take care of it.

Brad held the dress with the tips of his fingers, striding away. Rather than toss it in the trash barrel next to the back door, he kept on walking, disappearing around the corner of the building.

Tim's mouth fell open when his gaze flitted to the attic. There had been a silhouette in the window. His skin prickled while his heart hammered fast in his chest. Carly didn't see it, she was curled up in a ball on the deck, clutching at him.

Tim glanced up at the attic window again. Still as dark as ever. They hadn't made it up there yet to remove the rocking chair. His eyes narrowed into slits. That was going to be the next order of business when he went back in the house.

Chapter 11

Tim

Day 2

Tim looked over at Brad and rolled his eyes before turning back to watch the road ahead. Brad's fingers were flying sending a text message to Sophie. When they'd got back to the house the previous evening, Brad had tried to get her on the phone and by text but to no avail.

"Give her some time, Bro. She'll come around and if not, there's plenty of other fish in the sea." When Brad flashed him a scowl, Tim decided to change tactics. "Look, after we've lived in the house for a while and she'll see that she was being melodramatic. I agree, that something really weird happened yesterday when she was there, but everything will turn out fine. She'll change her tune when we start making some serious money."

"Somehow, I doubt that."

Tim's stomach lurched lower. "What? That we're going to make a go of this?" Jeeze! Was Brad having second thoughts on all of this? He flipped the turn signal, seeing the sign for Loughborough Road up ahead.

"No! Not that. We'll do great. No, it's Sophie. She's not into money. She's more about being happy, living a full and peaceful life." Brad's mouth pulled to the side and then he looked away at the fields they skimmed by.

"The two things are not mutually exclusive, you know." Tim took a deep breath, anxious to change the subject.

The day was overcast with heavy, grey clouds, threatening rain at any minute. There'd be no lunch on the dock or swimming that day. Which was just as well, since Carly had to work and it would only be the two of them at the house.

"Hey! What'd you do with the little girl's dress that was in the lake?"

Brad snorted. "What'd you think? I sure as hell didn't throw it out. I hung it up in the garage to dry. Not sure what we'll do with it but I'm sure we'll come up with something." He let out a small chuckle. "It sure scared Carly."

Tim felt his neck grow tight. "*Us too.* That must have been horrible for her. I can't imagine a worse death than drowning, man." His eyes narrowed. Clawing for air and feeling your lungs fill with water, ugh! When his number was up he hoped he died in his sleep. At the age of a hundred and ten.

The first day out there was anything but a picnic for any of them. First Sophie, then the taps turning on by themselves, Carly almost drowning and then that stupid rocking chair.. He could have sworn on a stack of bibles he'd seen it rocking when he looked up at the attic window.

But he'd taken care of that. The chair was now in the parlor, where it should be.

"You think the house will be ready for us to move into by the end of the month? I'm not sure we should have sublet the apartment so soon."

Tim wheeled the car down the lane and threw a scowl at Brad. "Four days? That's plenty of time. The fridge and stove arrive today, and after that, there's no advantage to staying in the apartment. We'll be on deck all the time and get more work done."

"I probably should buy my own car. Even an old clunker like Sophie's would do. I hate to see one of us stranded out here, in the middle of nowhere." Brad unhooked his seat belt and reached for the door handle. "Did I tell you what Sophie said when she stepped out of the car?"

Tim forced a smile, even though he wasn't the slightest bit interested in what she'd said.

"She said it was like stepping into pea soup. That's weird, huh?" Brad's eyebrows rose and he got out of the car.

"*She's* a little weird." He hurried along to the front door when a clap of thunder boomed across the sky. Maybe he should ask Carly if she had any girlfriends to hook Brad up with. This thing with Sophie was probably not going to work out.

When the door swung open, the results of their efforts the day before filled his nostrils. Instead of the usual musty smell, the scent of soap and pine drifted in the air and he breathed deeply—it smelled more homey already. They just needed pizza in the oven and the smell of stale beer. He listened but the only sound was silence, no hissing of taps spewing water.

"I guess we should tackle the top floor. Get our bedrooms ready at least." He walked through the arch to get the vacuum from the library, where Brad had left it the day before.

When he stepped into the parlour, he came to a grinding halt. The rocking chair was angled at the window, at the opposite end of the room from where he put it yesterday. His voice was low and he kept staring at the chair as he asked, "Brad? Did you move the rocking chair?"

Brad appeared next to him. "No. I wouldn't touch that thing if I didn't have to, not after the fright it gave me. Why?"

The pancakes he'd gobbled for breakfast, rose higher in his tight gut and he swallowed hard. But he couldn't let on to Brad. Not after Sophie's theatrics yesterday and Carly's skinny dip from hell. He grinned and continued on to the window. "It's nothing." He scowled at the chair and continued on to get the vacuum.

Hoisting the machine up the stairs, his heart started to race. That damned chair! He should break it up and build a bonfire.

His eyes closed for a moment and he shook his head. But that was the point wasn't it? The creepiness of the chair was what they'd wanted. If it mysteriously moved, then so what? It wasn't hurting him—not unless making his skin crawl off his body counted.

Actually, he could have some fun with this. Brad need never know. He'd move it and see where it ended up the next day. Under his breath he whispered. "How creative can you be, Mr. Ghosty?"

He started to laugh and had to pause at the landing at the top. Listen to him! Now he was playing games with the ghosts, talking to them! But after yesterday, he had to admit that something odd was happening.

"Are you all right?" Brad peered up at him from the bottom step. Hanging from his hand was a bucket of soapy water, where a yellow sponge bobbed up and down.

The sight of his friend, a veritable 'Mr. Clean' in the white T shirt and jeans, was comical. But it was the lumberjack hands in the bright pink gloves that really put him over the edge. Tim doubled over laughing, letting the vacuum slip from his fingers.

He fished in his pocket and held the cell phone high, taking a picture of Brad. He'd have to get it printed and frame it. Mr. Jock Macho McDude in pink rubber gloves.

He was still laughing, ignoring Brad's insults to his mother, when he clicked the button to see the photo. His smile vanished and he stopped breathing at what he saw. Oh my God.

"What? You think you're so funny, don't you!" Brad was thundering up the stairs, trying to hide the grin.

The photo showed Brad, but he wasn't alone. Above Brad's shoulder, the face of a bearded man was staring directly into the camera with narrow eyes, smiling. Actually, it was more like a menacing leer.

Tim's fingers shook, flying to erase the image before Brad got there. He clicked the trash bucket icon and it was gone.

He managed a smirk when he looked at Brad standing next to him. "Sorry Bro, it must have been too fast and in this lighting, nothing showed." Sucking in a gulp of air, he forced a cheerfulness he sure didn't feel. "Too bad. I was going to blow it up to poster size for a laugh. Maybe put it on Facebook."

He turned away and the smile fell from his lips picking up the vacuum. That pic made his blood turn cold. If *he* was creeped out, what would Brad have felt if he'd seen it? He'd put more credibility in what Sophie had said, that was for sure. Brad was skittish enough right now.

He shuddered and the food in his stomach roiled. Oh God. The fucking guy's face had been right next to Brad's.

The taunting grin lingered in his mind's eye. A trickle of cold sweat coursed down his spine. Sophie's words echoed in his brain. "Your house is possessed."

Chapter 12

Brad

Brad peered at his friend. Tim was never good at lying. If he was pretending he hadn't got the picture, and was going to post it later to embarrass the hell out of him...well....

Actually, Tim's face was pale and he had a strange expression. What the hell was bugging him now? Best to let it go. "C'mon. Let's get these rooms done. That is, if you're through goofing around."

Tim's eyes flitted to the foot of the stairs and then he turned to go up the last flight without saying a word.

Whatever. Tim was acting a little strange, though.

Brad lugged the bucket, the water sloshing in it almost going over the side as he followed his friend. "You know, I think we should set up the surveillance equipment before we move in. Being way up here at night, in the middle of nowhere...I'll sleep better if I know what's going on below. At least put them at the entries. Maybe we can set up a motion detection alarm."

Tim paused at the top step and turned to peer at him. "Yeah. I guess that makes sense."

"Hey! We were going to install them anyway. I just think we should do it sooner rather than later, that's all." Brad jerked his head to the side, indicating for Tim to keep going. The loneliness of the house, just the two of them living there alone for a month at the very least, was starting to bug him.

When they entered the first bedroom he set the bucket down and plucked his phone out of his pocket. They needed some music to break the stillness. Tomorrow he'd bring the speakers out but for today, they'd have to make do with the phone's sound system.

When Tim plugged the vacuum in, he put the phone back and walked over to the window to start there. He wiped the damp sponge over the glass, and years of dirt came off.

It might have been a good idea to take before and after pictures of the rooms. He'd mention it to Tim when he finished with the vacuum.

Outside the rain was a steady downpour, transforming the lake and dock into bleary gray sheets. There was a crack of thunder, a flash of lightning and suddenly, dark quiet enveloped the room.

"Well, that's it for the vacuuming for a while. The storm must have knocked the power out." Tim dropped the wand of the cleaner with a ringing thud. "And it's too dim to even sweep."

"Great. I wonder how long it'll be out." Brad tossed the sponge in the bucket and turned to face his friend.

A loud pounding broke the stillness. Both of them jumped, their eyes wide as dinner plates. Brad stood for a moment, like a deer in the headlights.

"HELLO?" A booming voice drifted up to the attic.

They both stared at each other in terror.

"HAALLOOOOO! Anybody there?"

"What the hell is that?" whispered Brad.

"ANYBODY HOME? Potter's Appliances!"

"Oh my God, it's the delivery guys. I'd forgotten about them." Tim turned and his feet were a fast drumbeat on the stairs.

Slowly, Brad started breathing again. He smiled. The place was so creepy that even a delivery guy had scared the hell out of him.

He picked up the bucket and walked down the stairs to join the others. From the window he passed, he saw the large white truck parked in the driveway, the rain still coming down in torrents.

When he stepped on the last stair, the hair on the back of his neck tingled and cold seeped into his chest. There was an odour that drifted in the air, like rotten meat. His stomach tightened and he breathed deeply through his mouth to keep from retching. Where was that stench coming from? Was there a dead raccoon in the walls?

Voices from the kitchen intruded into his senses. Taking two more steps, the smell disappeared. Oh God. Whatever was in the air in that spot was rank.

He noticed wet footprints on the floor and followed them to where Tim stood talking with a burly man in a blue shirt and pants, while a younger rail thin guy shifted from foot to foot watching them.

"If we give it a few minutes, it might let up a bit. That is...if you don't mind waiting." Tim smiled at the older man.

"You won't get any complaints from me." The guy looked around at the kitchen, from the cabinets to the floor. "Nice place you got here."

Brad slipped by them stepped over to one of the counters. When he turned, Tim's eyes met his, and he winked.

Tim leaned back against the counter and crossed his arms over his chest. "It's haunted."

The guy's eyes went wide and his mouth fell open. For the first time Brad noticed the name sewn over the pocket of his shirt. "Elroy". The man's gaze flitted between Brad and Tim and his head drew back.

The skinny guy stepped closer to his partner and looked around, over his shoulder. He looked like a scared rabbit, ready to bolt at any minute even though it was pouring outside.

Elroy cleared his throat and managed a tight smile. "Who told you that? I mean, how do you know it's haunted? Sure, it's old but that doesn't mean—"

BANG! The windows shook from the force of the thunder clap.

Now the skinny guy was so close to his partner that their arms touched. "Maybe, we should wait in the truck. We're keepin' these guys from—"

"No, no. It's fine. The power's out so we're kind of at a standstill anyway." The corners of Tim's mouth twitched in a smile. "Would you like a tour of the house?" He stepped closer to the two men, the personification of the friendly host. Mr. Carson in *Downton Abby* had nothing on Tim.

"Fuck off. This place isn't haunted. You're makin' this up." Elroy shook his head and gave his friend a dirty look, stepping away from him.

Once more, Tim glanced over at Brad. He'd been challenged and damned if Tim didn't love a challenge.

"A family was murdered in this house." He walked across the room and turned to beckon to Elroy and his helper. "C'mon. I've got something to show you...if you dare."

"Not me. I'll be out in the truck when you need me." The thin guy scampered past Tim and was out the front door like a shot.

Brad smiled when Elroy shrugged and followed Tim across the hallway. This was bound to be good. Brad followed them past the parlour and into the library, watching as Tim lifted one of the two books off the shelf.

"See this? It's a book about summoning the devil." He held up the copy of *The Alchemist* they had found in the garage. The previous owners used this. Who knows what evil they brought here, but whatever it was, it killed the whole family." He leaned in closer to the guy who was staring with golf ball eyes. "When we first looked at this house, this book was in a box in the greenhouse. When I came here yesterday, it was laying open on the table."

"Hmph." The older man tore his gaze from the book and looked at the floor for a moment. "But someone may have left it there without your knowing. That doesn't prove anything."

"That's true, I guess. But it doesn't explain how when we stepped outside yesterday, all of the cabinets were open and the faucets were turned on by themselves." Tim smiled, meeting Elroy's gaze.

"Get out!" Elroy's head jerked back. "Are you kidding me?"

Tim drew an 'X' over his chest. "Cross my heart. Every faucet, both on this floor and the upstairs bathroom were all turned on, and..." he leaned forward, *"nobody was in the house!"*

Elroy straightened up. He licked his lips. "You're full of it."

Tim turned, affecting an air of casual nonchalance, looking out the window. "I think it's cleared for a bit. Maybe we should move the stuff inside." He smiled at Brad and then turned once more to Elroy. "I'll help you if you want."

Brad's eyes narrowed as he watched Tim walk away, following closely on Elroy's heels. What was Tim up to? If anyone should be helping the guys it was him, not Tim. He was the fitness guru.

The lights flickered on and broke the gloom of the room. Well that was one thing at least. He walked back to the kitchen to get the cleaning bucket of soapy water. Above him, the vacuum whined, ready to finish the job. He shook his head; Tim forgot to turn off the switch when the power went out, that's all. He hoped.

Tim opened the front door and stepped to the side when the fridge appeared, perched on the dolly. When Elroy followed it into the house, he gave Brad an odd look before his gaze skimmed over the stairs.

Brad smiled and continued carrying the bucket up the broad staircase. Whatever else Tim had told the guy, had sure made a believer out of him. The nervous look in his eyes and quick movements hurrying to get the job done was plain to see.

He'd have to ask Tim about it later. It was bound to be something that they'd use again.

Chapter 13

That same day...
Sophie

She didn't know if her eyes were bloodshot and red rimmed from crying or from the lack of sleep. She shrugged the rain cape from her shoulders and carried it to the back room of the store.

When she returned to the main area, Aphra stood up from dusting the lower shelves of the Chakra display. Her deep brown eyes showed concern looking over at Sophie. "Did you find the newspaper article?"

Sophie nodded sadly and held out the copies she'd made. "There were a couple."

Taking the pages, Aphra adjusted her eyeglasses and read silently as Sophie watched her. At one point, Aphra's eyes widened, and a moment later she let out a quiet 'oh my'. She glanced up at Sophie, her mouth thin as she flipped to the second page. "Hon, go in the back and make a pot of tea."

Her hands rolled nervously over each other, clasped at her waist as she walked once more to the back room. The sense of dread that Sophie had felt since visiting Brad's new house, had only increased with her visit to the library at lunch. She needed some kava tea, pronto. Her hands shook as she plugged in the kettle and threw a couple of sachets into the porcelain teapot.

Aphra appeared at the door opening. "Sophie, from what you told me this morning and now this...it's worse than you thought. Those boys are in serious peril."

Sophie's eyes filled with tears. "Now I know what it was that I felt when I was there. I've never experienced anything sinister like it before. It's an ancient evil! That family...it killed them...it possessed the father and—"

Aphra stepped over and put her arms around Sophie, held her close while rubbing the base of her spine. "Easy child. Be still and let this negative energy flow out of you."

Sophie sighed and began to control her breathing. Before long she felt calming warmth fill her chest, as she drew from the serene strength of Aphra. She let herself be led to a cushioned chair and eased down into its depths.

"Deep cleansing breaths until you are at peace and then we'll talk. I'll get the tea." Aphra's voice was a soft, soothing balm.

Sophie inhaled, her palms cupped and turned up to gather the positive energy that pervaded the store. Gradually, she felt her thighs and neck muscles relax and grow warm. She opened her eyes and Aphra sat across from her, extending a small cup of tea.

"Feeling better?" When Sophie nodded, Aphra's hand seemed to float up and her fingertips grazed the centre of Sophie's forehead. A tranquil smile graced her lips and her eyes were soft, gazing at Sophie.

Sophie leaned forward, "I have to show this to him. If he sees these newspaper articles, he'll understand the nature of the power he's toying with and leave before it's too late."

Aphra's head tipped to the side and she looked down at her lap for a moment. "Maybe." She smiled sadly. "But I'm more inclined to believe that he won't."

"He *has* to!" Sophie jabbed a finger at the papers in Aphra's hand. "The evidence is right there!"

"Well... maybe..." Aphra lifted her head to look at Sophie. "But maybe not." Running her hand over the pages, she said, "He may... he probably *will* view this differently than you and I do."

"Now *that* would be close minded."

"Dearest, when you started seeing Brad, how did you describe yourselves to me?"

Sophie's mouth twitched. "Yin and Yang? Opposites?"

"You said that he looks upon himself as a skeptic, and sees you as an optimist. You're more open to the possibilities of the Universe, and he considers himself more grounded." Aphra laughed lightly. "Gods know I've tried to draw him out of his narrow views."

"Yes, but I don't think teasing him is a good strategy. He just becomes more and more convinced you're a space cadet!" Sophie couldn't suppress a smile.

Aphra waved her hand in the air. "Well... maybe I lay it on a little thick when he comes into the store, I'll grant you that." She sat opposite Sophie. "I do enjoy teasing him. I try to say the most ridiculous mystical things to get a rise out of him. But he's never once taken the bait. He's stubborn, and like most men his age, he's convinced he has the world figured out. No, Sophie. I think the best way you can help Brad is prayer, meditation and give him every amulet, crystal, healing herb that we can muster up for his protection."

Sophie sighed. "I'm going to stop at the church on my way home. I haven't been since I was a little girl but I'm calling in all markers. Holy water, crucifixes..." she grinned. "I'll be a walking talisman."

"Speaking of which..." Aphra twisted to the side and reached for a bundle of dried cedar, sweet grass and sage along with a large clam shell and lighter. "This can't hurt, either." She lit the end and a scented smoke rose from the dried herbs. Her hand drifted from Sophie's head, shoulders and down the length of her body. "If Brad comes over to your place tonight, do this for him."

As she continued the ritual, Aphra said, "I knew when I first met you that your third eye, your ability to perceive on another level was highly developed."

Sophie just nodded.

"But, I gather that this is not the first time that you've sensed entities beyond the veil."

Sophie finished her tea and inhaled the white smoke drifting in the air around her body. Immediately she felt refreshed and cleaner somehow. "My Grandmother was a sensitive. I must have inherited it from her." She let out a gentle laugh. "My mother wasn't at all, so it must skip a generation. Granny and I used to drive Mom crazy when we were all together. She and I knew each other's thoughts. We always partnered playing bridge and we were unbeatable."

"I'm talking about something wider than the connection between two kindred spirits, Sophie."

"I know you are, Aphra." Sophie frowned. "But the only other person I ever discussed it with was my Granny before she passed on." She took a deep breath and set the cup on the small table next to her.

"All my life, Granny and I were completely in sync. But after..." she fluttered her hands in the air and began to blush a little.

"After puberty set in..."

Sophie nodded. "Yes. Things changed and I was able to sense spirits. Not all the time, and not all that might be around me, but it became a regular occurrence." Her face tightened. "It was Granny that helped me cope with all of it."

"You were never afraid?"

"Of the spirits?" She shook her head. "No, not at all. It felt entirely natural for me when I began to sense them. It was like I was talking to someone in another room." She held out a hand. "What was frightening for me was when I tried to tell other people about it." She gave a small shrug. "Mom thought I was losing my mind." Pointing a finger for emphasis, she said, "Now my mother's response—that was scary. She totally freaked out." She let out a huff of air. "But when I spoke to Granny about it, she told me I had to keep that gift to myself, and I did."

Aphra leaned forward. "Well, I don't have the gift, but I *do* believe you, Sophie."

Sophie patted the woman's hands. "And I truly am grateful. I haven't told a soul about this since my Granny died."

"Do you hear them all the time?"

She shrugged. "The spirits I've seen sense that I'm attuned to them. Usually, I'm able to carry on and treat it like it's white noise. If I didn't I couldn't function." A smile flashed on her face. "Not always though. When I was in first year of college and rooming in an old house, there was a spirit that I had to help. It was either that or never get a full night's sleep again. A man who had been killed in a car crash, wandered the halls looking for his wife and daughters. He couldn't fathom that he was actually dead. I helped him cross the threshold to find peace."

"Amazing." Aphra's voice was barely a whisper, her eyes wide and intent staring at Sophie.

Sophie inhaled and shook her head slightly, dispelling the memory. "But now? There's no helping whatever is in Brad's house. It is better left alone." Her fingers knotted in her lap and she looked down. "I'm frightened Aphra. This thing has killed before and it *will kill* again!"

Chapter 14

Brad

Later that night, Brad knocked on Sophie's apartment door. She had finally replied to his text messages and phone calls late in the day, and even though he was bushed from all the work on the house, he couldn't wait to see her. Considering how she had lit out from the Inn, he was pretty surprised that she invited him over to her place at all.

He took a deep breath squaring his shoulders. She said she had learned some important information and wanted to show it to him. Well, whatever she'd found out was not going to spoil his plans...well his and Tim's plan. What did she expect him to do? Turn tail and run? Abandon his dream, because of her fear and superstition? Not to mention the fact that every penny in the world he had was tied up in the Inn and he was in debt up to his eyeballs with the mortgage.

Dammit! He gave up his career for this venture! She was in for a rude awakening if she thought she was going to change his mind with all her granola eating, New-Agey claptrap. Not going to happen.

In spite of his annoyance, when she answered the door, his heart did that familiar cartwheel. "Hi," he said. It came out like a croak from his suddenly dry mouth. Her cat like green eyes, and the smile on her cherub lips did what they had always done—made him go all pitter patter inside. Even after six months as a couple, even after waking up next to her on more than a few mornings, the first sight of her always turned him to jelly.

Dammit! Did she have to be so damn perfect? It wasn't fair. He loved her so much she annoyed the snot out of him sometimes. He took a deep breath and smiled at her. "I'm glad you asked me over," he said with a normal voice.

She brightened at him. "I'm glad you came. You've got to see what I found out." She grabbed his hand and pulled him inside.

He sighed as she led him across the room to the futon, the scent of cinnamon and cedar wafting through the room from the candles burning on the high armoire. The small indoor fountain gurgled like the brook back out at the Inn, and in the background a soft melody from a Pan flute gently twinkled from a speaker in the corner. With her artistic flair she could make even a basement bachelor apartment an enchanting oasis.

And she was dressed the part herself. Her gauzy mid eastern tunic was airy and loose over her black leggings. He wasn't sure, but he didn't think she had anything on underneath. She patted the seat next to her and he sat down.

"Sophie...I'm glad you finally answered my text. I'm really sorry about the way things went for you back at the Inn." His hand began to stroke her upper arm, as he leaned in to kiss her, but she turned her head at the last second.

"Hold on Brad, we need to talk. I left the property because I was scared out of my wits."

"Yeah, I know. Who blabbed to you about that place?"

Sophie looked puzzled. "Nobody told me a thing about that place. What I felt there was *from* that place, Brad!"

"Yeah, right."

"It's the truth!" She thumped her fist on his knee in frustration.

"Okay, okay! For the sake of argument, I'm not going to argue!"

She looked at him levelly and sighed. "What do you know about that house that you didn't want me to know about?"

He shrugged. "There was some sort of a murder that happened there. Some guy went crazy or something." He held out his hands. "That's why we were able to get such a great price for the place."

She shook her head. "That house has a really bad history, Brad."

He felt his heart sink lower. Of course he already knew what she was going to show him. The fact that the family had died there was not a negative as far as he and Tim were concerned. It was callous perhaps, but it was marketing. They could handle whatever crazy weird shit happened in the house.

"Okay. What did you find out? I'll warn you up front it probably won't change anything...." He perched on the edge of the futon, leaning over to see the newspaper article that she'd printed.

She elbowed him sharply and her eyes were narrow when she turned to face him. "Brad, I know you want to make some money off this but you guys don't know what you're fooling with." She tapped the page with a purple fingernail and continued. "Just read this. I'm sure this family thought the house was wonderful too."

He glanced over at her and sighed once more before starting to read.

The Kingston Whig Standard
September 12, 2001
Tragic Family Murder-Suicide

Ontario Provincial Police officers came upon a scene of tragedy and horror at 3155 Lakeside Avenue, on Thursday. The bodies of six family members, including four children, scattered around the large house, appeared to be the victims of a multiple murder-suicide, said Detective Sergeant, Mike Moran.

The family—a father, mother and four children—had not been seen the day before at work or school, and the father's co-workers had asked police to check on them, he said.

"This is a complex crime scene" that will take several days to sort through, Moran said.

He declined to release the victims' names, ages, or manner of death, or to speculate on why it happened.

The home, built in 1931, is on Loughborough Lake, near Kingston. It had been sold in August to husband and wife Joseph and Eleanor Baxter, according to Frontenac County property records. The couple have four children, two sons ages 12 and 4 and two daughters, ages 10 and 8, according to public records.

As evening fell, investigators from the Ontario Provincial police continued their work at the scene. The Frontenac County Medical Examiner's office was to conduct autopsies.

Scanner traffic between police and dispatchers indicated that all of the victims appeared to have died of severe injuries. After entering the home, officers secured a small dog, then began a search and found the bodies, one by one, in different areas of the house.

> Moran said he has never seen a scene so grim in his three decades of police work, and that finding the bodies was extremely difficult for the officers involved.
>
> "There're no words to describe it. ... It's a tragedy," he said. "This is a tough one to handle."

As he read, the sinking feeling grew heavier in his chest. The scrawled printing 'Jonas' flashed in his mind. Here was living proof of the poor kid's death. It could have been in that room, since the bodies were found all over the house. *Hearing* that there'd been a murder/suicide and actually *reading* the police account were waaay different experiences.

He sat quietly for a few moments and then slid the page away from him. "It's awful. I wonder why he killed his family. Fuck! Even the little guy, four years old? Why? He must have been schizophrenic or something. No one in their right mind would do such a horrible thing."

She placed her fingers on his hand and leaned closer. "That's just it. He wasn't in his right mind. Whatever is in that house must have broken him. Brad, that's what I sensed...that evil."

"Oh come on! You're telling me that there's some evil spirit in that house that made that guy do this?"

Sophie nodded. "I think it's somehow tied up with historic events, that it gets its power when something horrible happens in the world."

"What the hell is that supposed to mean?"

"Look at the date of the article, Brad," she tapped the top of the print out and peered up at him. "Baxter killed his family on 911!" She sat back on the futon. "I checked the timeline of that event, and I bet the killing started when the first plane was hijacked."

Brad sighed. "It's just a coincidence, Sophie. You're making some kind of a mystical conspiracy out of thin air."

"Well, the same thought occurred to me. So I kept digging." She produced another printout and handed it to him.

His stomach fell and his skin began to crawl as he read about a second family that died at the house. This time it was in the 1940's, and it was a family with only two children. He looked up at Sophie.

"The same name? Baxter?"

She nodded. "Look at the date, Brad." When he looked down and back up at her blankly, she let out a frustrated grunt. "Those murders happened on August 6th, 1945!"

"So?"

She sighed. "That morning, more than twenty thousand people died in the blink of an eye when Hiroshima was bombed!" She snapped her fingers. "Just like that! Twenty thousand people were vaporized! Loads more died that day from the fires and radiation, but it was the largest single instant of loss of life in history!" She snapped her fingers again. "Just! Like! That!"

The frozen chill that went down his spine told him there was something to this theory of hers. Both times 'Baxter'? Both times on enormously tragic days for humanity?

As if she was hearing his thoughts, Sophie said in an even voice, "These aren't coincidences, Brad. There's a connection." It drove him nuts when she did that. It was almost like she was reading his mind and he resented the invasion of privacy.

"But what? What's the connection?"

She shook her head. "I don't know! But I know that there is one!" Her eyes welled up.

Oh shit. His face was tight watching her, the concern in her eyes. It was on the tip of his tongue to tell her about Carly's incident and the dress. Sitting here, he knew that wasn't an accident. That thing tried to scare the hell out of her. But there was no way he was going to tell Sophie about it.

"How's Carly? What does she think?" asked Sophie.

"What the hell does she have to do with this!" he said, rattling the pages in his hand.

She flinched back. "I don't know. She just popped into my head, that's all."

This was going full speed into the Twilight Zone. He had to put a stop to it.

He sat back on the futon and turned towards her. "But this kind of thing happens all the time. You read it about it. Some guy or woman just goes crazy and kills everyone. Look at that woman in the States who drowned

her kids in the bath tub. You can't blame the house. It's
mental illness, that's all. Tragic but there you have it."

"Twice?"

"Sure! Crazy does run in some families you know."

Her chin drooped to her chest and her voice became
soft. "I knew you'd say something like that. But what I felt
when I got out of the car—that was *real*, not mental illness."
She turned to face him and her eyes were wide with earnest
when she spoke. "There's something evil in that house. I'm
really scared for you and Tim. You laugh about this stuff,
but it's real."

Brad had held his tongue, but his patience finally
broke. "Sophie! Stop it." His eyes closed for a moment and
he gritted his teeth. "I admit the place is creepy. Maybe there
is something to bad karma lingering, I don't know. But
we've bought the place and that's going to work for us, don't
you see?"

Her hand flashed out and she jabbed his chest.
"What I see are two idiots toying with some powerful stuff.
You're in over your heads and you're too dumb to know it."
Her fingers bunched in his shirt and she tugged him close.
"It's dangerous! You could be hurt or killed, asshole!"

He shoved her hand away and stood up. She'd gone
too far. "Enough with the evil spirit shit, okay?"

The fire in her eyes extinguished, to be replaced with
concern looking up at him. "God, I wish I could talk some
sense into you."

"SENSE INTO ME? Are you kidding? I'm the one
giving you reasonable explanations! You're the one who's
living in an episode of the X-Files!"

For a moment or two, all energy seemed to seep out of his body onto the floor. He'd never spoken to her like that before. She looked helpless and beaten down, her shoulders slumping and locks of auburn hair falling forward, all because she cared about him. He might not agree but he had to respect her concern. "I'm sorry, Sophie. Honest, we'll be okay." He reached for her hand, wishing that he could fold her in his arms and make everything better. But that only worked in the movies.

She grasped his fingers and stood up, giving his hand a good squeeze and looking straight into his eyes. "Will you do something for me?"

"As long as it doesn't involve selling the place before we've even got it off the ground, then sure."

A sad smile formed on her lips and she blinked a couple times to clear her eyes. She gave him one last squeeze and stepped away to the armoire. There was a small black box there next to the candle. She picked it up and turned to face him, lifting the lid off. "I got two of these today. The priest blessed them with holy water."

Over her fingers were two loops of silver chain and crosses that glinted in the soft candle light. "There's one for you and one for Tim. Please wear them."

"I don't know. I really don't believe in any of this stuff." He took the chain from her hand and held the cross looking at it. It wasn't just a cross; the figure of a man was fastened to it.

"It's a crucifix, a symbol of faith." Her gaze was soft looking into his eyes.

"Faith? I don't go to church—"

"Neither do I. But the priest who helped me pick them out—"

"Probably the most expensive ones." He muttered, handing it back to her.

Her hand flew up and she shook her head. "No! Keep it. It's an acknowledgement of power greater than ourselves—a power than can help you."

He snorted. "So, to protect myself I should wear an amulet of a dead guy?" A smile flashed on his face to soften his words. "I'll wear it, if only to please you."

Her lips were set and she reached for his hand, gripping it firmly and giving it a little shake. "No. Wear it to acknowledge a greater power..."

"You couldn't just do some feng-shui thing? Come out to the house and rearrange the furniture or something?" He laughed and ducked when her hand flew up to cuff his head.

"Eejit!" She smiled despite herself. "Look. I don't care if it's Catholic, Hindu or Wiccan. All faiths are unified in one concept, that there is an unseen power or force that is far greater than us."

"Yoda, you are not." He looked down to hide the laugh.

She jabbed her hands against his chest and took the chain from him, slipping it over his head. "Look, I may not be as new age as Aphra but I know there's more in the universe than meets the eye. Try to get Tim to wear his, okay?" Her hands cupped his face and she looked him in the eye. "This is important to me. I know about this stuff, all right?" When he nodded, she took the crucifix and slipped it over his head.

The serious tone and concern in her eye melted his last resolve. He'd wear this and do his best to get Tim to, as well.

Her hands slipped down from his face and rested lightly on his chest. He pulled her close and kissed her forehead. "I'm listening Sophie. I'll wear the crucifix and I promise I'll be careful. But you have to listen to me as well. Trust me, if you can. This will work out well and maybe down the road when you see that, it can be the way it was between us again."

She lifted her chin and her eyes met his. "I'll try to listen and respect your point of view, even if I don't agree. I want us to be together but I'll have to think long and hard about going out to the house to visit you. If you want to see me, you'll have to come here...at least for a while."

Brad's eyebrows rose and he smiled. It wasn't perfect but at least they were still together. At this point it looked like they were agreeing to disagree. He could live with that...for a while at least to see how it worked out. The thought of her not being a part of his life was just too depressing.

She grinned and rose on her tiptoes to kiss him lightly. "Maybe I should be giving you sweet grass..."

"I haven't smoked weed since high school" He shook his head watching her. What the hell?

"It's First Nation spirituality, smartass." She handed him Tim's box and her face was tight with worry again.

"Covering all your bases, huh? The next thing, you'll be calling a witch doctor with rattles and beads or something. Tim will definitely have a conniption over that." He pocketed the box and sighed. Tomorrow was another full day of work at the house. He really should be going, but still he lingered.

Her hand rose to rest lightly on his back. "I'll do whatever it takes, Brad, with or without Tim's approval." Her hands drifted to the buttons on his shirt and she smiled slipping them open.

Chapter 15

Tim
Day 3

Tim was perched on a stepladder, finishing the installation of the security camera at the front door. It was top of the line, with night vision capability and unlike the others to be installed inside, this one was triggered on by motion or sound.

He looked down from his perch to see Jeff Comstock, the contractor they hired, ease himself around the ladder and go to his panel truck. Tim didn't mind at all that Brad was the one to help the guy set up the electrical and plumbing for the washer and dryer. If he never had to go in the infested basement again, he'd be a happy camper.

He finished the last screw, checked the position of the sensors and camera lens and went down the ladder. As he bent over to put his tools and supplies back into the toolbox, the silver crucifix Sophie had sent him slipped out of the collar of his shirt.

Still kneeling on the floor, his fingers closed on the tiny object and rested there for a few moments. What was it about this amulet that made him feel a sense of calm from wearing it? He didn't believe in religion. It was probably the only thing he'd ever agree with Karl Marx on—that religion was the opiate of the masses. Still, there was no denying the fact that he liked wearing it. Brad had been surprised when he took it without any sarcastic remark.

Jeff the contractor grinned at him as he once more eased past the ladder. He was burdened by plumbing pipes and tools.

"Sorry, man," Tim said, standing. "Let me get that ladder out of the doorway." He felt a little abashed kneeling there lollygagging while there was still a lot of work to be done.

"Thanks, man," said Jeff, continuing on to where he was working.

Tim popped the braces on the ladder and slapped it closed. "Owww!" His finger got pinched between the steps and the support legs. He jerked his hand away, flicking a droplet of blood onto the wooden floor. Damn it. He stuck his finger in his mouth. Uh oh. When was the last time he'd had a tetanus shot?

He set the ladder on the wall beside the door and walked into the kitchen to run some water over the cut. He could hear the contractor and Brad down in the cellar banging away as they re-ran the pipes for the new appliances. Things were really starting to come together.

He put his finger under the tap and hissed at the sharp pain. After a minute he pulled his hand away, relieved at seeing the blood begin to clot. It might not get all of the germs out but at least he had a fighting chance.

There weren't any band-aids, so he grabbed a paper towel and wrapped his finger before heading back to the entrance to get the ladder. When he got there, he stopped short and his eyes narrowed. The ladder was halfway up the hall. In addition, while his toolbox was where he left it on the porch beside the door, the drill was perched on the top step of the ladder.

With the battery taken out and placed on the next lower step.

There were only the three of them in the house. He could still hear Brad and Jeff working in the cellar. Passing the ladder he went to the front door and looked down the driveway and across to the garage. As he suspected, he saw there was no one else around. His stomach tightened and he exhaled slowly.

When they'd arrived this morning, the rocking chair had been exactly where he'd left it. It was the first thing he'd checked when he walked into the house. It was funny because it had been kind of disappointing. But now, the ladder moving and the drill taken apart made his skin crawl. It felt personal somehow—the closeness of something moving stuff he'd just used. Without making a sound!

His finger started to throb painfully.

His jaw set and he took a deep breath before reassembling the battery and drill and dropping them into the tool caddy. He picked up the rest of the tools and walked back into the house. There were still three cameras to set up. Too bad the ghost, or spirit or whatever the hell it was, wouldn't help with that rather than play stupid pranks.

He walked down the hall and stopped when he came to Brad, coming up out of the cellar. "How's it going?"

"Good. The plumbing and electrical lines are set up downstairs. It's just the final hook-ups now." His gaze dropped to the wad of paper towel looped over Tim's finger. "What happened to you?"

"Nothing. I pinched my finger in the step ladder." He picked the paper away and looked down at his finger—as badly as it was throbbing, it had stopped bleeding. "I'm going upstairs to finish the cameras. Let me know if you need my help moving the appliances."

"As if..." Brad chuckled. Jeff came out of the cellar and the two of them looked at Tim's slender frame then each other and laughed.

"Screw you." Tim turned and went up the stairs and set the next camera and the drill on the floor in the hallway.

He went back downstairs to get the ladder from the hallway.

His breath froze in his chest. It was gone.

Even though his heart must have skipped twenty beats, he let out a huff of frustration. "Oh maaan!" he said. He went to the front door and stuck his head out.

The ladder was now at the *end* of the house, closed up, lying on its side and leaning against the wall. This was ridiculous. Once more he looked around the yard and down the driveway. But again, the only movement was a butterfly and a bird swooping by.

"Is that you, Baxter? You don't like the cameras? Well, fuck you."

Brad had filled him in about the Baxter family history in this place. He didn't give a damn if it was Baxter from the '40's or the Baxter from 911. Baxter was Baxter and he was starting to annoy him. He strode down the veranda and grabbed the ladder from where it was propped. Now, at least he had a name for the ghost, after Brad bringing home the newspaper article from Sophie's. It certainly was a gruesome story. What kind of maniac would kill his kids? Even the four year old?

When he stepped back inside carrying the ladder, he jumped, wide eyed at the series of thuds that boomed through the house.

They suddenly went silent, followed by a series of rasping scrapes in the walls.

Tim didn't move.

"Got it!" Jeff's voice called out and then the whine of an electric drill filled the air.

Of course, the hook-ups. He shook his head and continued up the stairs to the second floor. Once he had the inside cameras set up, he'd turn them on and let them run for the night. He could test the recordings with his laptop tomorrow to make sure they worked.

He set the ladder up and placed the camera on the top before grabbing the drill and climbing up. The camera would pick up any movement down the hallways, to the back of the house.

As he secured the electronic device to the ceiling his face grew tight. After seeing the face in the picture he'd taken the day before, there might be weird things showing up on the recording that they weren't counting on. That face yesterday had only been the beginning. Then the drawers and faucets, and now the crap going on with the ladder?

He blinked. Carly's encounter with that dress in the lake wasn't any fluke. He didn't know what to call that incident, but it was more deliberate than random, that was for sure.

Things were starting to heat up, and he was getting more concerned. Especially considering they'd be actually living in the house in another day.

He put the last screw in and tested the camera's stability. Solid as a rock. It wasn't going anywhere and neither were he and Brad. If the recording showed ghostly images, so much the better. Maybe he could post them on You Tube and make some money out of it. It could be their film debut. They might even get a movie deal out of it.

He stepped off the ladder and wiped his hands on his jeans. Two more to go.

Chapter 16

Tim
Day 4

Tim arrived by himself the next day. Brad was visiting a car dealer and Carly had agreed to pick him up and bring him out to the house when he was through.

He grabbed the laptop and got out of the car. It was almost the end of July, a perfect summer day and he whistled as he strode across the veranda to slip the key in the lock. He had to be quick. He only had an hour or so to view the recordings from the video cameras before Carly and Brad would arrive.

The house was quiet as a tomb when he stepped inside. And the air was once more a bit musty smelling and cool on his skin. His footsteps echoed off the walls as he walked through the dining room to set the laptop on the kitchen counter.

His skin crawled. It felt too quiet. He whistled a faint tune as he climbed the stairs to get the memory card from the camera. When he walked down the stairs, he got the card from the camera in the hallway and went back into the kitchen.

In no time flat he was opening the program to view the video recordings. The screen filled with a daylight scene of the long hallways bordering the stairwell. Everything was as he'd left it. He took a deep breath and then sighed long and slow. Of course that would be the case.

The recording covered a span of fourteen hours. There was no way he had the time to stand there and view all of that. He clicked a button and the fast forward function kicked on, although it was hard to tell, other than the light gradually fading as night fell. He stood watching the screen for another few minutes, seeing only darkness. He paused the action to record the time. The small timer at the bottom of the screen showed twelve, twenty-four.

At least the fast forward was humming right along. At this rate, he'd only have to watch for another ten minutes to get to the end of it. He clicked the icon to get the thing moving again.

He settled his butt against the counter and folded his arms over his chest looking at the dark screen. This was almost as boring as watching paint dry. Suddenly the screen flashed a few times, like a strobe light, revealing the hallways...and...

His heart lurched up into his throat. Oh my God. He leaned over and hit the pause button, then rewind. When the screen showed again it was in real time speed. The light in the hallway flashed on and off repeatedly. But the real spooky thing was seeing the doors to the bedrooms. Each one of them slowly opened and then banged shut with a force that shook the floor, jiggling the image out of focus for a second.

He hit stop and then replayed it another time, staring at it as his heart beat fast in his chest. He kept watching, barely able to breathe, even when the screen once more was dark and nothing seemed to be happening. His finger pressed the fast forward button and he peered at the laptop, waiting for something else.

At the sudden creaking noise coming from the other side of the house, his head swivelled around. He stopped the recording with a trembling finger and stepped away from the counter, cocking his ear. The creak was slow and steady.

He tiptoed across the floor, through the dining room and into the parlour. The sound was louder and at the movement in his peripheral sight, he turned to look into the library. He froze, heart thundering in his chest, while his lungs locked.

The rocking chair was next to the window, and it was swaying back and forth. Perched on the seat, at the edge was the alchemy book, splayed open. The chair rocked slowly and came to an abrupt halt, throwing the book to the floor with a sharp thud.

He jumped and his eyes bulged from his head, fixated on the book and the now immobile chair. What the hell!

He forced himself to take a deep breath, followed by another and another. His heart slowed down although his body felt like he'd just run a marathon, weak and jittery. Holy shit, that was scary.

He breathed a sigh of relief when he heard a car in the driveway, followed by the banging sound of car doors slamming shut. Thank God, they were here.

He looked over at the book laying open on the floor and the rocker sitting still. His jaw clenched tight and his hands formed fists, the nails of his hand biting into his flesh. Whatever had just happened had scared the shit out of him! He'd have to check his underwear later. A nervous laugh erupted from his throat.

"Think you're pretty good, huh Baxter? I have to admit, you had me there for a minute. But I'm not a four year old kid you're dealing with you *bastard*. Ha! The joke's on you. You're going to make me a millionaire." He smiled a tight lipped grin and turned to greet Carly and Brad who were just entering the house.

"How'd you make out? Find a car, Brad?" He grinned, hoping his voice sounded natural. His body still tingled with fright.

"Yeah. There's a Subaru that's not too bad. I'm picking it up tomorrow." Brad looked around and turned puzzled eyes to him. "Where's the paint? What have you been doing? Slacking off, I bet."

Tim stepped to Carly and kissed her lightly. "Hey doll. Thanks for giving asshole a lift." He turned and walked into the dining room, calling over his shoulder, "I left the paint for you, muscle man. Hop to it."

He kept going to the kitchen, ignoring Brad's insult to his ancestry. He had to get the memory cards from the laptop and hide them. He paused for a moment and his lips were tight. Maybe he should show them to Brad. They'd be moving in the next day and at least he'd be a bit better prepared.

He took a deep breath and snapped the laptop lid shut. No. He'd mention the lights flickering and doors banging but the actual footage was too eerie. Best to ease him in a bit at a time. It was creepy, not life threatening. They could handle this.

***

He was in the house, running from room to room, looking for her. Carly sounded scared and hurt. He raced up the stairs, pivoting fast around the newel post at the top. The lights were flickering on and off and doors were opening and then banging shut with a force that was deafening. Where was she?

His heart raced and a bead of cold sweat trickled down his spine, when he entered the first bedroom. It was empty and the tree branch tapped wildly at the window. He scurried back out and stopped in horror, seeing the barrel-chested man leering at him, coming closer while his hand gripped the axe tight.

The words wouldn't come. Somehow he was struck dumb for a few moments. Finally, like pulling his voice from the bottom of a well, he barked, "Where is she?"

"She's mine." He was so close now, the fine veins in his bloodshot eyes and individual hairs in his beard showed. "Challenge me, eh? Just remember, I drew first blood." He raised the axe.

"NO!" Tim shot up in bed, his heart racing hard in his chest, looking around the room.

When a warm hand touched his arm, he jumped.

"It's okay, Tim. It was just a dream." Carly sat up and put her arm around him.

He was still shaking, the face that he'd first seen in the photo with Brad was etched in his brain. His finger throbbed like a son of a bitch and he looked down at it. A droplet of blood had seeped through the band aid circling his finger.

First blood?

Chapter 17

Brad
Day Five

Brad turned down the lane leading to the house. It was almost noon and he was late getting there. The car business had taken longer than expected and the beer store was crammed with people stocking up for the long holiday weekend. His fingers thrummed on the steering wheel as he wheeled the new car in beside the rental, moving van.

He noticed Tony's jeep, and Carly's rust box Ford beside a blue Malibu parked close to the garage. The Malibu must be Tim's friend Steve from work. He'd met him a couple of times and liked him right away.

"Hey slacker. Got the new wheels, I see." Tim yelled at him, but only his head and hand could be seen next to the mattress he was helping unload from the van.

"Yeah. Pretty sweet, huh?" He stopped and watched Tim manhandle the mattress, almost losing his footing walking backward down the ramp. "I'll get the coolers and load 'em up with beer. First things first, Bro."

He turned and went back to the car to begin the bar set up. With all the free help, the least they could do was supply the booze and food. With any luck, they'd be done by five and start the bonfire.

Carly appeared next to him and smiled. "I'm not much help with the heavy stuff. Why don't you let me handle this?"

"Be my guest." Sure she could figure it out; her day job was working in a bar, after all. He grinned and handed her the car keys. "I was thinking of setting the coolers on the end of the veranda. We can build the bonfire next to the lake and set up there. You might want to drive the car closer, to save your back, lugging stuff."

She grinned and took the keys, scampering over to the car. Carly was actually pretty nice and unlike Tim's other girlfriends, she had some common sense. She wasn't afraid of getting her hands dirty and working as hard as the rest of them. Just don't put a mouse anywhere near her. Yeah, he liked her.

He wandered over to the van and stepped onto the metal ramp. Tony, their friend from university was lifting an upholstered leather chair from the pile of furniture. His T shirt was stretched tight over a wide chest and the muscles of his arms bulged from his efforts. Brad had seen this many times before at the gym, where they often partnered with the weights.

"Hey Tony! Let me help you with that." He stepped forward and grabbed the side of the chair.

"Brad! Nice place, you guys got here. I'm going to be visiting you a lot with my kayak." He nodded to the other side of the chair and then squatted to pick up his end.

"Thanks. Yeah, anytime you want. Did Liz come with you today?" It was a silly question. When the couple weren't at work, they were usually inseparable.

"She's inside, helping get the kitchen and bedrooms set up. She likes organizing stuff. She'll probably write up a list and post it on the fridge for you. She's got my underwear and socks colour coded, I swear."

"We really appreciate you guys helping out like this, man." Brad smiled and stepped backward, the chair firmly in his grasp.

"Any excuse for a party works for me." He pivoted his head taking in their surroundings. "Hell, we may never leave, it's so nice out here." Tony laughed and they continued the rest of the way up to the veranda and into the house.

Tim and Steve were just coming down the stairs, the sweat dripping off their foreheads and soaking their T shirts.

Brad and Tony manoeuvred the chair into the parlour. "Yeah, we'll have to get a ton more of furniture to fill this place up. There's an antique place not far from here that's overstocked and pretty reasonable. We want to maintain a sort of old school, antique kind of atmosphere as much as we can."

Tony stopped in his tracks as they crossed into the parlour. "Whoa! Do you feel that?" Tony looked across at him, the whites showing around his chocolate brown eyes.

"What? I don't feel nothing but aching muscles." He jerked his head to the far wall. "Over there, I think."

Tony set the chair down and rubbed his hands over his bare arms. "You didn't get a chill? Seriously, when I stepped into the room, it felt like a freezer. I don't mind cooling off but that was a too intense for my liking."

Brad smiled and clapped his friend on the back. "When we first saw the place with the realtor, we noticed it too. Maybe I'm immune to it now. The place is *supposed* to be haunted, right?"

Tony's smile fell from his lips and his forehead furrowed. "Wait a minute." He tilted his head. "I thought that was a scam. But maybe not, huh?" He hurried from the room and out the door.

When Brad followed him into the truck, Tony turned and looked at the floor for a moment. His eyes were serious when he looked up. "You sure you guys know what you're doing? The place is nice but, Dude, that totally weirded me out."

Brad decided to ignore the clench in his gut. "That, my friend is what we'll get the big bucks for. Weird is our bread and butter."

Tony picked up a cardboard box and handed it to him. "Well, all I can say is I'm glad it's daytime and I don't have to spend the night here. I grew up with haunted houses, you know."

"What do you mean?"

Tony grabbed another box. "My grandparents' house was creepy and when they died they left the place to my folks and we moved in. Man, it never stopped. Things would go missing, lights turning on by themselves and that awful feeling that someone was watching you all the time."

Brad laughed. "Where is it? Maybe we'll buy it and set up a franchise of haunted houses across the country." He turned and trudged down the ramp.

"Hey dude, it wasn't funny. *It was weird.*"

Carly walked across the veranda just as he reached the door. "The bar's set. I'm going to look for branches and wood for the bonfire. I've been dying to wander along that stream since I saw it."

"Knock yourself out. It's going to take us at least another hour to empty the van." Brad brushed by her and into the house. He took the box into the kitchen and set it on the counter.

Liz's blonde head popped up from where she squatted next to a cabinet. "Hey Brad. Whaddaya' got there?"

"Dishes." He smiled and extended a hand to help her to her feet. Her arm was lean and muscled from all the time at the gym with Tony. "Thanks for helping like this."

"Are you kidding? I can't wait to tell everyone at work I was in a real haunted house. They'll be so jealous!" She laughed and flipped the lid of the box off. "Seriously, I'd like to be your first customer!"

Brad's eyebrows bounced high. "You'll have to do it alone then. Tony's too much of a wuss to stay. The place has already freaked him out. And there's no way we'd charge you to stay. You know that, right?"

She plucked the bubble wrap from the top of the box and began taking the plates out. "Honestly, I'm going to really talk the place up for you. I'd love to arrange a party with the girls at work. Maybe do a séance or something? I noticed the Ouija board in the library." Her broad smile and glinting blue eyes underscored her excitement.

"That sounds cool." He stared at her silently for a moment. The possibilities for making money with the house were limitless it seemed. If only Sophie could see it like that. Even if she wasn't working that day, he doubted that she would have come out to help with the move. She was still pretty nervous about them being in the house.

***

As expected it was just about five p.m. when the truck was unloaded and the house was more or less organized. Well, the beds were made and they'd rummage in the kitchen in the morning, figuring out Liz's system of organization.

The day had been a scorcher and the lake was cool. Brad swam out about twenty feet from the dock, enjoying the coldness of the deeper water. Tim's arms flashed high, swimming out to meet him. The others paddled close to the dock and yelled before jumping and canon-balling off the end of it.

"Hey! The move went pretty well, huh?" Tim treaded water and smiled looking over at him.

"Yeah. I can hardly believe we're spending the night here." He dipped down and took a mouthful of water, spraying it high in the air at his friend.

Tim ducked to the side and continued. "About that, Brad..."

"What? We're not spending the night?" Tim was acting quiet and mysterious now. His neck muscles tightened. What was he up to? Maybe a raucous night with Carly and forewarning him about that?

"You know the cameras..." He looked away for a moment and then turned his eyes to him once more. "Things happen at night in the house." From the set of his mouth, no smile, Tim was totally serious.

Goose bumps spread like lice under his skin. "What things?" He glanced over at Tony and back to Tim.

"There's no easy way to say this, so I'll just say it." His mouth clapped shut for a second. "The lights flicker on and off and doors open and then bang shut." His eyes were wide, waiting for Brad to answer.

For a few seconds Brad couldn't speak. His heart had picked up speed and he gulped air, trying to stay afloat. With narrow eyes, he pulled through the water to get closer to Tim. "You saw that on the memory card? You didn't think maybe *I* needed to see that?" He splashed water into Tim's face. "Last time I checked *my* name was on the deed too!"

Tim's eyes were wide peering at him. "It's not like that! We're partners, okay?" His face fell. "But sometimes I feel like I might have talked you into this."

He swam over and placed his hands on Tim's shoulders, pushing him under the water.

When Tim arched away and came sputtering to the surface, there was fire in his eyes. "What was that for, asshole?"

"For not levelling with me, jerk! For thinking you're smarter than me, that you could *talk me into* this crazy scheme." He splashed him once more. "Honestly, I should hit you. You didn't talk me into this. I'm not as stupid as you think I am, asshole." He shook his head from side to side. "So it's haunted! We kind of *knew* that, right? We'll deal with it. But we have to be upfront and honest with each other. No secrets."

Tim's nodded. "Okay, no secrets." A small smile twitched his lips and he chuckled. "You thought that the noise from my bedroom was bad, with the girlfriends?" He gave a short laugh. "It ain't got nothin' on what happens in *this* house!"

"No shit?" Brad wished he'd had a chance to see the video. "Just don't try to climb into my bed if you're scared, okay? Send Carly if you want, but you're on your own, buddy." He laughed and together they swam back to their friends.

Tim grabbed the side of the dock and pulled himself up."Anyone who drinks too much and wants to spend the night, is welcome. You may have to sleep on the sofa but it's better than driving drunk."

"No way, man! You couldn't *pay* me to sleep here. Scared straight? Try scared sober!" Tony shook his head and emptied the rest of his beer in the lake.

Liz looked over at Tim and Brad. "I wish we could. But, I'll get a gang of my friends together and we'll christen the place."

A horn sounded and another car pulled into the driveway.

"That'll be Sylvia and her friend. She couldn't be here earlier but she's dying to see the place. You don't mind do you?" Steve got up and looked at them before heading away from the dock.

Tim looked over at Brad and waggled his eyebrows. "Hmm...A friend. This could be interesting Brad."

Brad's shoulders slumped and he grabbed the side of the dock. The only girl he'd be interested seeing there was Sophie. But she was too frightened of whatever was in this place to come. And there was something in this place. He definitely knew that now. He fingered the crucifix dangling around his neck.

Chapter 18

Tim

Tim towelled off and went up to the bonfire where Carly was standing. "You're pretty quiet. Is something wrong?"

She threw another branch into the roaring flames and glanced at him. "It's nothing..." She gave her head a small shake. "I don't know."

"What's nothing? Tell me." He pulled her close and planted a wet kiss on her cheek. The fire felt good after being in the lake.

She looked up at him and tucked a stray tendril of hair behind her ear. "When I went to get wood for the fire, I thought I saw something funny by the stream." She shrugged. "It was probably my imagination."

"What do you mean *funny*? What was it?" He gazed into the flames, thinking of the white object he'd seen that first day in the copse of woods lining the brook. There had been something there. He was sure of it and now Carly had seen it too?

He glanced down at Carly. "If it's any consolation, I saw something odd there the first day we came. I caught something white out of the corner of my eye and then it vanished."

She pulled away and shook her head. "No. That wasn't it. I thought I saw a man. For just a split second, then he just vanished. It made me nervous so I came back and grabbed wood closer to the shore."

Tim shivered and his gut became a tight, empty gourd. "What did he look like? How old?"

She looked into his eyes."Maybe fifty or so and he had this heavy, black beard.

Tim's chest froze and the smile dropped from his lips. "Carly?" He sighed and edged in closer to her. "I think that might have been the resident ghost, Baxter. He and his family were the last people to live in this house....and die here. A grisly, murder suicide thing."

Her head fell to the side and she looked up at him with narrow eyes. "Gee, after the first day, with the taps turned on by themselves, I had a pretty good idea that the place was haunted. And now, I just saw the actual ghost?"

"Yeah...maybe." He held his breath waiting for her to answer. Would she be weirded out like Tony? He watched her face soften and a grin form on her lips.

"Cool!" She grinned and then turned to look into the flames. "So you may not need me to be the ghost?"

"Hey! I didn't say that. Who knows if this ghost or whatever it is, will ever show when we have guests? We need to ensure that we put on a show. So, yeah, we'll still need you." It was hard to believe but, watching her by the fire, he felt his heart ache at the prospect of her not being there.

He shook his head, watching the fire. HIM of all people! Tim the Player Holland, falling for a waitress.

"You still have to pay me for the appearances...even though we're sleeping together. I'm trying to get some money together to go to the east coast. I've never been and I

121

want to be there by winter." She nudged him with her shoulder and grinned. "I'm dying to see Newfoundland, you know."

"Of course you'll be paid, Carly! We already agreed on that, right?"

She nodded. "Just confirming."

He sighed inwardly. Yeah, he'd help her get the money together so she can leave him.

Tony and Liz wandered over to the fire, leaning over and holding their hands out close to the blaze. From the look on Tony's face he wasn't too happy.

"Is that offer still open? To stay the night?" Liz's eyes were bright, rubbing her hands together.

He looked at Tony, his lips a straight line. It was obvious that Liz was strong arming him on this. "Sure. Drink as much as you like and go home in the morning."

"I'm perfectly fine driving home after we eat." Tony cast a hard look over at her.

She sidled up to him, looping her arm through his and tugging him closer. "Please. It'll be fun. I've never stayed in a haunted house. I can't wait. I packed a sleeping bag just in case. It could be cool."

"You're nuts. Trust me, it's not fun." He stepped away, trying to slough away from her grasp.

"Wuss! Don't worry. I'll protect you." Her chin jutted out and she stood straight, openly daring him.

Tim's eyes darted back and forth between them, aware that he was walking a tightrope whatever he said. Thankfully, Carly spoke up.

"I'm staying tonight, too. C'mon Tony. It's not like you'll be alone or anything. There's plenty of room and we can have a big feast in the morning. It's the long weekend. C'mon." She grinned at him and her eyes flashed to Liz.

"I'm not sleeping in the parlour." His voice was reluctant and low.

Liz's eyes lit up and she quivered, she was so excited. "We'll sleep in one of the bedrooms. Maybe the yellow one overlooking the lake. We could have a séance later!"

"No! I'm not staying if you do that." Tony wandered off to the cooler of beer and grabbed a couple bottles. "If I'm staying, I might as well get some more liquid courage."

It was odd. Tim felt relieved that they were going to stay the night. Who knew what would happen later, after seeing the memory card and what happened when no one was in the house?

He looked over at the veranda when Brad, carrying a platter of hamburger patties and buns appeared in the doorway. "Start the barbeque, Bro. We're starving."

Tim put his arm around Carly and pulled her close. The day was warm, the lake pristine and cool, with lots of beer, food and good friends—a perfect move-in party. He looked at the house, from the lazy veranda spread around the solid stone walls, the high rounded windows and the top two dormers, like eyes looking over the lake.

His new home *and* a ticket to a better life. Tonight would be their first night there, a trial run. Liz would be like most of their customers, anxious to be scared silly. He huffed a sigh and smiled. Are you up for that, Baxter, you demented prick?

Chapter 19

Tim

Sitting next to the fire, Tim glanced at his watch—twelve twenty. Almost time for the action inside the house to start, if the video was any indication. In the recordings he'd viewed, it had happened at twelve twenty-four each night.

There were only the five of them still left, finishing their beer, making noises like they were ready to call it a night. Even though Carly had tried to get Steve, Sylvia and Amy to stay, they'd begged off for another time.

Tony was half lit, stumbling back from the edge of the property after taking a leak, while Liz had stopped drinking a few hours ago. She didn't want to miss a minute of what might take place in the house.

"I'll get the sleeping bags and pillows from the car." Liz stood up and stretched, stifling a yawn before she disappeared into the blackness of the night.

Brad got up and turned to Tony. "If you two want to take my bed, I'm fine with that. There's no air mattress and why should *two* people suffer on the hard floor?"

"Are you sure? I'm fine sleeping in the car. I don't know how she talked me into this." Tony sighed and suppressed a loud belch.

"No problem. I'll take the front bedroom." Brad stepped close to Tony and clapped him on the back, walking close to him all the way into the house. From the look he shot over his shoulder at Tim, it was clear he was there in case Tony needed a hand navigating.

Tim looked up at the second floor. It was still dark, no light-show yet. He sighed, disappointment vying with...Oh my God. He shook his head. Relief? Really? What the hell was wrong with him? He should be hoping for some action in the house! It was *supposed* to be haunted.

When Carly stood up, he pushed his weary body up off the ground to join her. The fire had turned to embers, with little risk of spreading beyond the stones circling it. She slipped her hand into his and they walked across the veranda. Liz, with her arms circling sleeping bags and pillows met them at the door.

Brad stepped close to her and took the sleeping stuff from her arms. "You and Tony are taking my bed. I'll bunk down with this stuff, but I might actually take the sofa, rather than the front bedroom."

Carly sprinted up the staircase, calling over her shoulder. "I'll get the lights up here. C'mon Liz."

Tim watched Tony follow them and he turned to Brad. "That's pretty nice of you, Bro. You sure you'll be all right down here by yourself?" He glanced into the dark parlour and back to Brad. Everything was quiet down there...too quiet. And the room was right next to the library and that damned rocking chair.

Brad rolled his eyes and he stepped into the dim room, flipping the light switch on as he went. "I'll be fine. I'm so tired, I can sleep through anything. I'm half in the bag too from drinking all night long. See you in the morning."

Tim locked the door and flipped off the outside light before turning and following the others up the stairs. He looked down the dark hallways and his eyes narrowed for a moment. Still nothing. It had to be almost one o'clock in the morning. Maybe all the life in the building had scared old Baxter away.

He headed for last set of stairs just as the door to the room where Liz and Tony were staying closed with a snick. Well that was Tony and Liz settled. He opened the door to his own bedroom, in time to see Carly slip on an over-sized T shirt. She tugged the comforter back and settled into the queen sized bed, patting the spot next to her and smiling up at him. All thoughts of haunting and ghosts evaporated with the welcome sight of her— waiting and wanton.

With a quick tug, his own shirt was off. His fingers fumbled with the snap on his shorts.

BANG!

He jumped at the thundering boom from the floor below him. His eyes locked with hers, the breath caught in his hammering chest. It was happening! Another loud bang and then another shook the floor under his feet.

He snapped the pants shut again and raced to the door. When he opened it, the lights downstairs in the hallway were flashing on and off like strobes at a concert. He barely dared to breathe as he watched the staccato light show, his mind numb with shock.

There was a pattern to the flashes. Three short, three long times on and then three short light flashes. SOS?

Liz peeked out the crack of the door to Brad's room. "Is it happening?" Her eyes were wide and the fingers holding the door were pressed flat.

Just as he was about to tell her to go back inside, a deafening boom shook the house. He froze. The door slammed shut and Liz disappeared inside.

But Carly stepped out to join him. "Holy shit! This is crazy!" Her eyes glittered above a gaping mouth.

"Stay here. I'm going down to take a look." He gripped her arm and squeezed it to make sure she got the point.

"No way! I'm coming with you." She clutched his hand and her jaw set tight. Her whole body looked like a coiled spring.

The lights downstairs turned off, leaving a chasm of darkness that he slowly stepped down to enter.

"What the hell's happening?" Brad's voice across from him sounded totally shit scared.

Tim took a long quivery breath stepping into the hallway, his hand scrabbling over the wall to find the light switch. When light flooded the area, his ragged breath slowly escaped. He looked over at Brad, who was white as a ghost. "Get the flashlight. I'm going to check all the rooms but I don't trust these lights to stay on."

Carly squeezed his hand and huddled close to him. "This is amazing!" At the sound of footsteps behind, she turned and beckoned Liz to join them.

All the while, Brad's feet slapped the wooden stairs, racing down to get the flashlight in the kitchen. Liz took her position on Tim's other side, her fingers digging into his bare arm.

"Do you think we'll see anything? A ghost I mean?" Her eyes were big as marbles, staring at him.

Below them, Brad's feet pounded on the floor, racing from the kitchen.

Tim took a deep breath. This was what he'd signed up for and—

"Holy shit!" Brad's yell broke the silence.

"What?" Tim stepped over to the top stair and looked down, his two charges clinging to his arms.

Brad strode back to the stairwell, taking the stairs two at a time as he climbed. "That damn rocking chair! It moved! It's in front of the sofa now, going like crazy!" He came to a halt on the top stair, his eyes wide staring at the three of them. "It wasn't there when I came up here! I *hate* that stupid chair!"

Tim felt his skin pucker in a shiver of goose bumps. This was seriously weird. "Sleep up here tonight. You can take the floor in my room or your own."

From the doorway behind them, Tony's voice boomed. "He can have his fucking bed back! I'm fucking out of here. You stupid fucks, fucking around with this fucking shit! C'mon Liz! We're fucking leaving!" Tony's feet thudded quickly on the stairs.

Liz spun around and took a step closer to him. "No! Wait Tony! We're going to check out the bedrooms. We can't—"

"Oh yes we can! We're fucking outta here. Or at least I am, with or without you!" Tony pushed his way by Brad and raced down the stairs.

Liz's forehead wrinkled and her teeth pressed into her lower lip. "Shit!" She eased by Brad, running down the stairs after Tony.

"Well, that solves the bed situation." The bang of the front door closing punctuated Tim's comment. "He'll probably never speak to us again."

Tim took the flashlight from Brad and walked over to the bathroom, easing the door open and creeping inside. He could feel Carly right behind him, her breath on the back of his neck.

Everything looked normal enough. Nothing in there but what should be there. He turned and with a flip of his hand, signalled for the others to step back. There was probably nothing up there, just empty rooms, but checking everything was the sensible thing to do, just in case. Although why *he* had to take the lead and not Brad didn't seem fair.

He crept down the hall to the next room, the pink rose one. When he stepped inside, it was like his dream the night before. The maple tree branch scraped the glass, the broad leaves spread out like a handprint. The beer in his gut threatened to spew and he took a deep breath.

It wasn't until they'd entered the bedroom at the front, the one with the huge stain on the floor that he saw something that made his blood turn to ice. Beside him, Carly gasped and her hand shot up to cover her mouth.

In the middle of the dark patch of wood, lay what was left of a mouse. It was a headless carcass, the skin peeled back from the upper part of its torso. It lay on its side in a pool of blood.

Tim's stomach tightened and the beer rose as bile in the back of his throat. This mouse had been left as a warning and he knew who had left it.

"Eew!" Carly turned and fled past Brad, hurrying out of the room.

Brad turned to watch her go, his hand still on the door, holding it open. "Oh shit." His voice was barely more than a whisper.

"What?" Tim stepped closer, his eyes following to where Brad peered. High on the back of the door, directly in the middle was a rust coloured drawing, a happy face symbol painted with blood, heavy drips rolling down from the corners of the smile.

Brad turned to Tim and he whispered, "Maybe Sophie's right."

Chapter 20

Brad
Day 6

Brad was the first one up the next morning. With the sunshine pouring like honey through the windows, the night before seemed like only a dream. His feet brushed the smooth wooden floor in the hallway leading to the front bedroom. He opened the door slowly and peeked inside.

Eeew! A cluster of oily, fat flies covered the carcass, their movement making it seem like the body was alive and rippling.

At the sound of footsteps on the floor above, he left the room and hurried to the bathroom. He grabbed a piece of paper towel and scampered back to remove the disgusting carcass. Carly would be up soon and there was no way he wanted her to see *that* again.

As he was about to round the newel post and go down the stairs, Tim's voice stopped him. "So it really did happen, didn't it? You got the mouse?"

He grimaced and held the paper towel out. "Yeah. I'll throw it in the field." He started down the stairs and stopped. "What do you suppose happened to its head?"

Tim snorted. "As long as it's not in my cereal, who cares?"

"Isn't that a pleasant thought..." Brad continued down the stairs. He walked by the entrance of the parlour and purposely kept his eyes averted. One thing at a time. If the chair was still there, he'd deal with that later. He crossed the driveway and went about fifty feet across the field, before throwing the mouse to the wind. Some hawk would probably have a nice breakfast.

He was bone tired, trudging back to the house. Everything had quieted down after they'd found the mouse, but sleep had been a long time coming. Having ghosts bang around and play with the lights was one thing but that mouse...There was something threatening about what had happened to it and then that happy face drawing cinched it.

When he went inside, he saw Tim manhandle the rocking chair back into the library. Was this the way all of their nights were going to be? Being kept awake almost all night, rearranging furniture in the morning and getting rid of small, animal sacrifices? Was this worth it? If it was, he'd better make an afternoon nap part of his daily schedule.

He went into the powder room and turned on the tap to wash his hands. At first the water sputtered and then a stream of rusty water spewed forth. Rusty to the point of looking like dried blood. He sighed and shook his head, hands gripping the pedestal sink. After a minute or so, the water cleared and he exhaled slowly. When he put his hands under the water, he drew back with a start. Holy cow! It was scalding!

He adjusted the lever and waited a moment or two. Still pretty warm but bearable. He'd have to watch that, especially if he was in the shower. After finding that mouse, maybe the ghost was playing with the water temperature and could seriously hurt them. He would go down into the cellar and turn the hot water temperature down. *He'd* have to do that, since Tim refused to enter the 'bowels of the building'.

When he left the bathroom, he went into the kitchen. Carly was pouring coffee while Tim cracked eggs into a frying pan. The normalcy of the situation struck him between the eyes. Looking at this scene of domestic bliss, you'd never know that last night had happened.

Tim looked over at him and said, "I'm going to town and get the stuff for the chute. I'm picturing something like a slide you'd see in a kids' playground, big enough for Carly to slide through, hidden behind the stairwell and ending up in the basement."

Brad's head dropped forward and he blinked a few times. He could hardly believe his ears. All the banging and the light show weren't enough for Tim? He wanted to add to the ambiance with a ghostly appearance from Carly, who'd disappear suddenly, down a chute? "Tim? Do you think that's necessary? After last night?"

Tim dished the eggs onto a plate and handed it to him. "Absolutely. Who knows how long Baxter will stay? Maybe he maxed out his ghosties with the mouse last night. We've got to make sure our guests get some bang for their buck." He popped bread into the toaster and continued. "It was something else though, wasn't it? I mean aside from the mutilated mouse."

"Eeew!" Carly's nose crinkled and she handed Tim a cup of coffee. Her wide blue eyes met his and she smiled. "Thanks for getting rid of it. I've always hated mice but what happened to that little guy was awful. Poor thing."

She took the milk from the fridge and reached for the sugar bowl, setting both next to his plate. "You'd never know I grew up on a farm, the youngest of three. We used to play in the hay and make forts there. There was always mice, even with three barn cats."

"Where was that, Carly?" Brad took a bite of egg and smiled at her.

"Elora. It's a small town near Niagara Falls. When my older brother and sister left the farm, our parents sold it." She sighed and dark hair cupped her cheeks when she looked down at the counter for a moment. "They're dead now and I haven't seen my brother and sister in years. They're corporate types and look at me...a high school drop-out. I always wanted to travel more than anything else."

Brad's stomach fell looking over at her. Sure, he didn't see much of his family but at least no one was dead.

Carly was a bit of a gypsy all right, flighty, but with guts. She'd have to be, to strike out on her own like that. "You're following your dream. Nothing wrong with that."

She smiled and turned to Tim. "I have to work tonight. They texted me that one of the full time girls called in sick. I'll be leaving the same time as you. I want to go home and have a nap, after last night."

He nodded and continued cooking breakfast. "How about you, Brad? What are you planning today?"

It was absolutely glorious outside, a typical, hot summer day. It would be wonderful to lay on the dock and grab forty winks in the sun. But that wouldn't help them get the place ready for guests.

He managed a smile. "I thought I'd tackle the dining room. It'd be nice to get it painted, so we can get the table and finish that room. I should be done by the time you get back. I can help you with the chute then. "

Tim glanced over at him and puffed a sigh. "I texted Tony earlier. He hasn't replied yet. Maybe I'll call him when I get back."

Brad finished the eggs, As he walked the plate to the sink to rinse it, he glanced at Tim. "Leave Tony to me. I'm better than you at kissing ass. I'll call him in an hour or so."

***

He was alone in the house, the paint, brushes and rollers set on canvas, drop cloths. It was deadly quiet and he needed some music or the radio to break the stillness. But that could wait.

He fished his cell phone from his shirt pocket and clicked the buttons to connect with Tony. He might as well get it over with before he got started with the painting.

"Hello?" Tony sounded like he had just woke up, even though it was almost eleven.

"Hey Tony. How're you doing?" He wandered over to the window and looked out at the expanse of overgrown lawn.

"Fine, no thanks to you and your fucking house." His words were clipped.

"Yeah...sorry about that. We should have let you go home like you'd planned. Things quieted down after you left but—"

"But what? You guys are okay, aren't you?" Anger was replaced with concern in Tony's voice.

Brad felt his chest lighten. Tony would come around. "Yeah, yeah. We're fine. The mouse we found didn't do so well—"

"What happened?"

He sighed and the eggs scrambled some more in his stomach. "There was a mutilated mouse on the floor in one of the bedrooms. And a happy face message painted with its blood."

"Fuck off! You're not serious?"

He hesitated for a moment before answering, "Yeah, I am."

"Brad, that's a threat. You know that, right? You're not dealing with a playful spirit there."

He could picture the worry in Tony's eyes. Kind of like the look Sophie had given him. "Yeah, that's what Sophie said too."

"She said that? Oh my God. Look I don't know her all that well but I think she's right. What exactly did she say?"

Brad turned and propped his butt on the window ledge, staring across the room. "Well, when she visited, she wouldn't come inside the house. She said the house is possessed, evil even."

"Holy shit!"

"Holy, all right. She gave us crucifixes on a chain and insisted we wear them." He fingered the chain around his neck, pulling out the cross. For some reason, having it in his hand gave him a sense of security.

"Brad, are you wearing it?"

"Maybe..."

"Seriously man?" Tony's voice blasted in his ear.

"Yeah. I am."

"Just make sure you keep wearing it. And get one for Carly too. She's out there a lot isn't she?" There was a pause and then Tony continued. "Brad, forget this scheme. Sell the place and get out while you can. I can't say it was a bad idea, but you've got the wrong house. There must be other old places that you could set up in. Listen to Sophie, if not me."

Brad stood straight and squared his shoulders. "Look Tony, I appreciate your concern but we can handle this. I'll admit that before I was in this house, I thought that ghosts and haunting were kind of bullshit. But there's been too many things that's happened here to say that now. But really, if you think about it, the house is perfect for what we're planning. We'll just have to get used to living in a haunted house. You said it yourself...you lived in spooky houses growing up and yet *you* survived it."

"That was different, Brad. Those ghosts were annoying but they didn't threaten us. Not like what's going on in your house. Maybe you should get a priest in there to bless the place. Send the bad spirits back to where they belong."

Brad's eyes closed and he gripped the phone tightly in his hand. That was never going to happen. Even if Tim agreed to it, there was no way, *he* would. They needed the ghost or whatever the hell 'Baxter' was. "We'll think about it, okay? I'd better get going. I just wanted to call and make sure you're all right. Again, I'm sorry about last night."

"Don't toy with this thing, Brad. You're making a mistake."

Brad clicked the phone off and wandered over to the parlour to plug his phone into the sound system. Immediately, the house was filled with 'Pretty Reckless' belting out their hard, stomping beat. Great music to get you moving and get the dining room painted.

He went back into the dining room and poured the cream coloured paint into the tray. As he rolled the paint he moved in time to the music, lost in the song and the brighter transformation of the wall. Just as he was about to start the side where beams of sunshine poured through the window, the music stopped.

His head swivelled to look over at the parlour, his lips parted, mid-lyric. Now what? He turned to peer into the kitchen, at the microwave. The green light showing the time was still on so it hadn't been a power failure. Was the battery in his phone dead?

Faint musical notes, like a piano would make, drifted in the air. The hair on the back of his neck spiked and he stood rooted to the spot. It was coming from the cellar—the same notes played over and over, the tune an old familiar one. His eyes closed and he took a deep breath, resisting the lyrics he'd learned in both English and French. 'Frere Jacques/Are you sleeping?'— a song from primary school?

He jumped when the stereo speakers blasted a crashing beat, dropping the paint roller and spattering his legs with white droplets. "Shit!" He picked the roller up and tossed it on the tray of paint. His teeth grit tight together, striding from the room and out the front door. This was ridiculous!

The music continued to blare behind him as he marched to the lake. He kicked his sandals off and sat on the edge of the dock, dangling his feet in the water. Would he ever get used to the shit that happened in that house? He leaned over and washed the paint off his calves, huffing a sigh. He was tired. They'd been working like Trojans for over a week and after last night...He didn't have the patience for that crazy shit, not today.

He sat back and rested his hands on the dock behind him, gazing up at the sky. Just fifteen minutes was all he needed, some peace and quiet sitting in the sun. Relax, do some deep breathing. He swung his legs from the water and shifted so that he laid on his back, soaking up the hot summer day.

He jerked upright at the touch on his shoulder. Tim's face came into focus above him. "Hey! What the hell happened to the dining room?"

Brad sat up straining his eyes wide to get the sleep out of them. "What time is it?" But even as he asked, he noticed the sun midway on the horizon.

"A little past two. What'd you do? Take a break and nod off?" Tim stood straight again and sighed. "If I wasn't so bagged, I'd be pissed at you. C'mon. Help me get the stuff out of the car."

He blinked a couple times, and got to his feet, feeling the tautness of his skin, burned from the noonday sun. The slow heavy gait of his friend, walking up the lawn made him feel guilty for a moment. He took a deep breath and stretched his arms over his head before hurrying to catch up with Tim.

"Hey! Wait up!" He came alongside Tim and looked over at him. "Remember that piano down in the basement?"

Tim's eyes narrowed. "Yeah?"

"Apparently whatever is in the house didn't like my music. They cut the sound and played a tune on the piano, *Frere Jacques*." Even though his tone was light, the memory of the song was eerie, etched in his brain.

Tim shook his head and his lips were tight. "That doesn't sound like Baxter. That's a kid's song." He opened the hatch of the SUV and reached in for the curve of white plastic. "Maybe there's more than one ghost in this place. One of the children, possibly?"

Brad nodded and took the piece of equipment from Tim. "Could be. I mean, they died violently, didn't they? Isn't that supposed to make them linger or something?"

Tim straightened up. "You're asking me?" he said, pointing at his own chest. "Who's the guy dating the Wiccy Wizard girl, man?" He turned his head and looked over at the house silently for a moment. "And the lights flashing on and off. Three short, three long and three short flashes again. S.O.S. Maybe, the wife is sending a signal. She probably tried to save her kids that night, right?"

"Yeah, but what the hell does 'Save Our Ship' have to do with anything?"

Tim's jaw dropped. "You're kidding me, right?"

Brad shrugged. "What?"

Now Tim's finger jabbed into Brad's chest. "Don't you know anything?" He waved his hand at the house. "They were saying 'Save Our Souls' dude!" His face grew pale, and he turned his head to the house. "Save Our Souls," he said in a whisper.

"You think so, man?"

Tim nodded. "And the doors..." he turned back to Brad. "They weren't trying to scare us..."

Brad nodded, his voice now also quiet. "They were running for their lives!"

"Or being chased..."

They both stood shoulder to shoulder now and gazed at the house. Tim's voice was low. "I think that every night, those murders take place over and over again...

The chill that went up Brad's spine told him his buddy was right on the money. "What the hell do we do about that?"

"We make a fortune from it." Tim smiled and reached into the car and pulled out two picture frames. "I got the articles that Sophie gave you framed, what do you think?

Brad nodded. If they were going to make a go of this plan, a nightly *for real* ghost haunting would be just the thing that would put them on the map. The wheels in his head started turning as he admired the objects in Tim's hands.

Looking up at his buddy, he said, "I think they look awesome. We'll hang them right at the front door." He smiled.

Chapter 21

Brad

By the time Brad finished painting the dining room, it was close to seven. He cleaned the brushes and roller and put everything away in the corner of the room. Everything was much brighter with the fresh coat of paint and he hadn't done a bad job, if he did say so himself.

Every blow of the hammer, Tim beating the chisel into the plaster, pounded behind his eyes. That, and the smell of paint was giving him a terrific headache. He walked over to the kitchen sink and poured a glass of water before rummaging through the cabinets for a bottle of aspirin or ibuprofen. He spied them on top of the fridge and tossed a few tablets back into his throat.

He climbed the stairs to see how Tim was making out. He'd made fairly good progress. Most of the plaster below the slope of the top stairs was gone, leaving diagonal strips of lathe. The area to be opened was a square, about twenty-eight inches on all sides— wide enough that when done, a slender woman could fit through easily.

At the light tap on his shoulder, Tim startled and his head spun around. He looked like an insect alien creature in the goggles and paper mask, his normally dark hair dusted white.

"I'm going for a swim to cool off and get clean. Are you just about done here for the day?" Brad squatted down next to Tim, gazing at the ancient craftsmanship of the house in the wooden slats and sturdy pine studs.

"Yeah, I think so. At least the dusty part is done. I'll need the Sawzall from here on out. We're lucky, there're no wires crossing this area." He set the tools down and sucked in a deep breath, getting to his feet. "I'm so tired, that I don't mind knocking off early. I'll join you for a swim."

Brad got up and grabbed a couple bath towels from the bathroom. Tim was sweeping hunks of plaster and dust into a dustpan as he passed by. "Okay. See you out there."

He went into the kitchen and slipped a couple of beer inside the towel and continued on his way to the dock. Even after the nap earlier that day, his muscles were heavy as lead. He felt fifty-six, not twenty-six and probably looked it as well. He peeled off the T-shirt and set everything on the dock before diving into the smooth surface of the lake.

The cool water took his breath away at first but after a few moments, it seemed to recharge his energy level. He surfaced and kept swimming until he was about thirty feet out. When he turned Tim was just stepping onto the dock and making a running leap to join him in the water.

"I brought a couple of beers. I don't know about you but I intend on drinking enough to let me sleep or pass out. If the banging starts up, I want to sleep right through it." Brad swam back, watching Tim tread water.

"I hear ya. There's still lots of burgers and beer left over from yesterday. We'll build a bonfire and do a rinse and repeat of last night." Tim fell into a slow breast stroke beside him.

The air was still warm and humid on his skin when Brad popped up onto the dock. That beer was gonna go down real smooth. He popped the caps and handed one to Tim when he pulled himself out of the water.

"To our haunted house." He held up his bottle and clinked it against Tim's.

"To Baxter helping us make money!" Tim laughed and downed half of it in one long swallow. "God, that was good!"

Brad looped the towel over his neck wandering off the dock on his way to the fire pit. "Let's get this thing going again. Then I'm going in to change and bring out the rest of that beer."

"Get the beer first. I'll work on the fire." Tim looked over at the house and yelled. "Hear that Baxter? We're having a bon fire and you're not invited, you sick bastard!"

Brad's eyes narrowed. "Hmph!" He'd second that emotion. If not for Baxter, they wouldn't be so tired. And what was with that shit with the music? The ghost or whatever couldn't leave it alone, even in the daylight? Weren't spooky things supposed to just happen at night? He finished the rest of the beer in one long swallow.

"Okay. I'll be right back. I might as well fill the cooler and bring it out. Maybe, I'll blast the stereo for good measure." He strode across the veranda and into the house. Everything was quiet as a mouse.

In ten minutes he hefted the cooler in his arms, the sound system belting out heavy rock behind him. The orange tongues of flames met his eyes across the lawn where Tim stood poking the fire, sending smoke and sparks high into the night. The sun was completely hidden under the horizon and the faint light, made the fire even more inviting. A draw as primal as man himself.

He handed Tim another beer and got one for himself. "Baxter is quite upset that we're out here. He left a 'sad face' on the bathroom door."

Tim's head jerked back and his mouth dropped.

"Just kidding." He laughed and grabbed a lawn chair to flop down into. "I talked to Tony. I think he's gonna be okay with us."

"That's good." Tim grinned. "I never knew that a sentence could contain so many fucks. Noun, verb, adjective, adverb. He's got a real flair with words. Should have been a writer."

"Or a sailor." Brad looked over at the house and chuckled. "I keep waiting for the music to stop or the lights to start flashing. But I suppose it's early."

Tim took a big swig of beer and looked at his watch. "Yeah. Baxter shows up at twelve twenty-four. That's why I don't think the piano was him." He paused and looked over at Brad silently for a few moments. "I saw his face, you know."

"What?" Brad's face knotted. "Where?"

"Remember that day I was teasing you about the rubber gloves and I took your picture before you came upstairs?" He looked away for a moment, gazing into the flames.

"Yeah?" Brad clutched the beer bottle tightly, watching his friend with narrow eyes. He had known that Tim was lying that day.

Tim sighed and sat back further in the chair. "His face showed up right next to yours, looking over your shoulder."

"What! Kind of like a selfie pic of me and Baxter?" He shuddered recalling the coldness in that spot. Now he knew why.

Tim laughed and slapped his thigh. "Yeah. Exactly. Baxter must be pretty vain, never missing a photo op. I kind of wish I hadn't erased it now. We could have posted it on our website."

"Website? Do we have a website now?" Brad shook his head and finished the rest of the beer off. It tasted like another one. He got up and lifted two more from the cooler.

"Not yet, but we will. Don't worry, I'm sure we'll get another pic of the two of you. But next time, turn your head at the last minute and pucker up. That ought to be a good shot. Wonder how the sick fuck would like that?" He turned and yelled over at the house. "How 'bout it Baxter? A Bro-mance pic? Would you like that?"

The music stopped abruptly. The sounds of crickets and a lovesick bullfrog's croak drifted in the still air.

Brad turned to Tim with wide eyes. "Guess he doesn't like the idea."

"Seriously, do you think that's why the music stopped?"

"Is this some drunken kind of séance thing? Say something else and see what happens."

Tim's eyes sparked and he grinned. "Hey Baxter! Put the music back on. Brad wants to ask you to dance. But make sure you do the strobe lighting thing. He's into that disco beat." He laughed and held his beer before his mouth, waiting for something, anything.

When there was nothing he finished the rest of his beer and started on another. "We should eat soon. I'm starting to feel this beer, man."

"I think Baxter's sulking in there. That trick with the music was supposed to scare us." The beer was cold and smooth and Brad was tired of being scared. His teeth grit together thinking of how many times he'd been creeped out since coming to the house. "Hey Baxter! Turn the music back on! If you *can*!"

Tim laughed softly. "Good one. Let's see what he does."

They watched in silence for a few minutes and Brad was just about to get up to throw another log into the fire, when the whole house lit up. Lights blazed from every window and the music blared louder than before.

"Whoa! *That* was pretty good." Tim sat forward and smiled.

Brad's heart had just about jumped from his chest. He stood up and continued stoking the fire. "Now what?"

"Finish your beer and grab a couple more. I say we go join the party. We're not through with old Baxter yet, not by a long shot."

Chapter 22

Tim

Tim led the way across the veranda and into the house. The ear-splitting music thundered in his gut, right down to his toes. He walked into the parlour and turned the volume down, stifling the chuckle that rose in his throat. "Think you're scaring us, Baxter? I think you'll have to do better than that—an electrical surge? That's the best you got?"

Brad stood in the entranceway, holding a beer out to Tim. "Don't forget what a mouser he is. He must have been a cat in a former life." When Tim took the beer, he continued, "No! He's not a mouser! Baxter's a PUSSY!"

The rocking chair that was sitting in the library began to rock back and forth, picking up speed as it went.

Tim glanced over at Brad and his eyebrows rose high. "Now you've done it, Brad. Baxter didn't like that crack." He turned back to peer at the chair, the hoops of wood clacking furiously on the floor. "You're like a spoiled kid, Baxter—throwing a tantrum because we're not sufficiently impressed with your tricks."

As if it was shot from a catapult, the chair skittered across the floor right at Tim. It would have banged into his shins had he not reached out to stop it. If that had happened yesterday, he might have crapped himself from fright, but today, he snorted, more than ready to call out the bully.

"Whoa!" Brad laughed. "Good catch, Bro! He sure didn't like that comment." He took a long swig of his beer.

148

"Yeah, the truth hurts, I guess. Baxter's trying to show off for us, Brad." Tim stepped around to the front of the chair and sat down. "Now let's see what you can do, Baxter? Ready to take me for a spin? Give us your best. Maybe we can charge a buck for a ride in the haunted chair."

Brad shook his head. "He can't move it now. Not with you in it. He's only good for killing little kids and moving empty chairs. Baxter's a real light-weight of a ghost."

Tim felt the chair start to vibrate, the sensation churning the beer in his gut. One hand gripped the bottle of beer while the other held tight to the arm of the chair. He grinned at Brad. "He's trying to, man; I can feel the chair vibrating. Can he do it, is the question."

Brad's eyes were narrow with laughter. "He's a little girly ghost. He can't do it. You're boring us Baxter." He nudged Tim's arm. "Do you want me to make us a couple sandwiches?" He turned and ambled out of the room towards the kitchen.

Tim let out a loud belch and stood. Turning to the chair he gave an effusive bow. "Thanks for coming out, Baxter. Sorry you didn't make the cut."

He wandered into the kitchen to stand watching Brad slather four pieces of bread with peanut butter. Aside from the music from the stereo system, the house was quiet. The lights in the kitchen and dining room were steady, glowing soft white. "I've got the feeling that's all the spooky stuff we'll see tonight. I guess he didn't like us making fun of him."

Brad slapped two slice together and handed one over. "The opposite of fear is humour."

"The resident Psych major speaks." Tim smiled and took a big bite of the sandwich.

"Jerk. What I mean is, we *can* control this thing. Honestly, the thought of spooky shit happening every night while we're trying to get this place ready for guests is exhausting. We need our sleep. When it's just us, we taunt it into submission. When we have guests, we show some respect and entice Baxter out."

Tim gulped the bite of food down and grinned. He turned to look up at the ceiling and dining room. "Hear that, Baxter? None of your nonsense tonight! We'll let you know when we need you, okay? Until then, dial the ghost shit way down."

Nothing happened. He turned to Brad and grinned. "Just call me ghost whisperer."

Chapter 23

Tim
Day 7

The next day dawned with overcast grey skies and the temperature had dropped a few degrees. Tim found himself actually pulling the duvet over his body and snuggling in. The sounds of birds chirping outside and the smell of bacon wakened him more and more with each breath.

He sat up and tossed the covers back, slipping his feet into his sandals and standing straight to stretch the warm loose muscles to life. Amazing what a good night's sleep could do to improve your outlook and energy level, even after downing so many beers the night before.

After stopping in the bathroom he trudged slowly down the stairs and into the kitchen. Brad was whistling some nameless tune, flipping pieces of bacon over. When he turned to face him, there was a sly grin on his face. "Guess we showed Baxter who's boss, didn't we?"

Tim stepped over to the counter and poured a cup of coffee. "Sure did! I just hope we weren't too hard on him and chased him off. We still need the old skuzzball."

"Maybe not. Remember, we'll still have the chute and Carly playing ghost. It might be more like our original plan to create the haunted experience. And, if it means we get a decent night's sleep and control everything, that's probably a good thing."

Tim took a sip of coffee watching Brad lay the crispy bacon on a paper towel to soak up the grease. His mouth pulled to the side and he sighed. Hard to believe, but he'd actually miss Baxter, if the ghost had moved on to God knows where old ghosts go. It hadn't been much of a challenge to put him in his place. Just like any bully, he crumpled when someone stood up to him.

He took a deep breath. "Speaking of which, I think today's a good day to finish installing the chute. If the two of us work at it, we should be able to get it done." He looked around the kitchen. "We're going to need it, especially if Baxter has split."

Brad nodded and nibbled at a piece of bacon. "When's Carly coming out?"

Tim smiled picturing her. He still couldn't get over how much he liked her, and her just a waitress—but a sexy, smart one. "I talked to her last night. She's coming out around dinner time." He held the coffee mug in both hands, leaning his butt against the counter.

"Great. We'll be able to test it tonight then." Brad finished his coffee and then turned to rinse his mug. "After that nonsense with Baxter, I'd rather not depend on him to entertain the guests. Things were pretty quiet overnight."

Tim nodded and plopped some bacon into his mouth. Yeah, maybe too quiet? Had Baxter moved on to another plane as these ghost fans claimed was possible? Not exactly slipping silently away...more like being laughed out of the room. They'd have to wait and see.

At any rate, getting a good night's sleep had its advantages. He felt like he could finish the chute and then start working on the electronics to make doors slam shut with the push of a button.

Brad set his dishes in the dishwasher and casually wandered from the kitchen, calling over his shoulder, "I'll get started upstairs." He stopped and turned to face Tim. "When are you setting up the website? I'd like to have some guests lined up before I hand in my notice at work."

Tim gave a short wave of his hand. "The website won't take much time. I want to do some trial runs after we get the chute and electronics finished. That way we can take videos and post them on the site."

"Yeah, you're right. I'm getting ahead of ourselves, I guess." Brad grinned and looked around the room. "You know? I think the house is starting to feel like home. I wonder if the old bastard is really gone now?"

Tim let out a guffaw. "Yeah! Exorcism with beer and heavy metal music! Who woulda' thunk it!"

***

Later that day, Tim stepped out of the bathroom feeling like a new man. Actually more like his corporate self, the clam digger shorts replaced with cotton trousers, the T shirt for a button down shirt, but he refused to compromise on the sandals. He whistled a tune as he walked down the stairs to join Brad. The cell phone in his shirt pocket vibrated and he scooped it out.

"RUNNING LATE. JUST LEAVING WITH THE PIZZA NOW."

His sighed. He was anxious to show her their work and even test it out. Plus he was starving. He walked into the kitchen and looked over at Brad. "Carly will be here any minute."

Brad had showered all the dust and grime from their work installing the chute but he still wore torn, but clean blue jeans. Despite the casual way he leaned against the counter, his face was worried. "Do you think we went too far last night? I mean, here we are, the place is supposed to be haunted and we've scared the ghost away?"

"No worries. I've got the proof right here for the website." Tim took an envelope from a shelf over the sink and dumped the contents onto the counter. There were five memory cards scattered like poker chips. "It's all here, date and time stamped. From the couple nights before we moved in to last night. The first night we stayed here, is the best, with Tony and Liz running out and the three of us finding the dead mouse. I took a few pics of the happy face."

At the sound of a car horn, Tim turned and walked to the front door. A wide grin spread on his face at the flash of car headlights and the banging car door. At last and not a minute too soon. He was starved.

A half hour later the pizza and half a bottle of wine was gone. Tim turned to Carly while Brad cleaned up, grabbing plates and glasses and stacking them into the dishwasher. "I can't wait to show you the trap door and chute. Honestly, you can't tell it's even there."

He stood up and reached for her hand, dragging her from her perch on the counter. "C'mon."

"I don't know about this. I'm not a big fan of closed spaces. I thought I'd have a bit longer to get used to the idea." Her voice was just a bit whiney, and her feet moved like molasses.

"It'll be fine. Brad and I both tested it. Think we'd let you try something we weren't completely sure was safe? Think of it like jumping into a mound of hay. Seriously, just a second or two and you're at the bottom." He turned and grinned to reassure her. What was wrong with her that she was getting cold feet on this? It had been part of the plan from the get go.

She stood beside him looking at the trap door. "You did a good job disguising it. I wouldn't know it was there if I didn't know you'd spent the day installing it."

He bent over and pushed on the door, so that it disappeared inside leaving a semi circle of darkness above the brighter shade of the plastic tubing.

"It's actually kind of fun." Brad stepped over to them and grinned. "Just hold your breath and enjoy the thrill! It's like a carnival ride."

"I don't know." Her teeth bit down on her lower lip and she stepped back. "Can't we do this in the morning? Maybe the first time should be in the daylight. This place is too creepy at night."

Tim looked over at Brad, both of them on the same train of thought. There was no need to go into what they'd gone through with Baxter last night. Actually the thought of relating it to someone sober and who hadn't been there was a little embarrassing. They taunted a ghost? Who would ever believe it?

"Look, there's nothing to it. Let me show you. I'll go first." Brad stepped closer and gripped the side of the opening, sliding his body into the tube. "Geronimo!" He disappeared down the tube with a whoosh.

Carly bent over trying to see into the dark tube.

"C'mon Carly! I'll catch you." Brad's voice boomed up through the opening.

Carly's nose wrinkled and she gazed over at Tim. "Do I have to?"

Tim scowled at her. "At some point you're going to have to. The first time is the worst. Look, I'll go next. I'll be down there when you come through." He swung his legs into the opening and grinned before letting his fingers leave the frame surrounding the hole.

It was easy and quick, the smooth surface of the chute hugging his body lightly. Near the bottom, the chute levelled out to slow the descent. He popped out and smiled at Brad. They both yelled up the chute. "Your turn, Carly!"

"We'll be right here to catch you!"

Brad looked over at him and rolled his eyes.

A rustle sounded hollowly above them and then her shout. "Here I come!"

A blood curdling scream pierced the silence.

Tim's breath caught in his throat. The scream stopped as abruptly as it had started. He bent over looking up the tube. The sole of her sandals came into view, followed by her thighs, the bright sundress bunched high. She slowed to a halt.

What the hell? He reached in to grab her foot. "Carly?" He pulled her body forward until her legs flopped out the end of the chute. Her eyes were wide and there was no sign of life. "CARLY!"

"Gotcha!" Her eyes crinkled and peals of laughter filled the room. Her hands lifted to grip the edge of the chute and pull herself forward. "Actually, you were right. It's kind of fun."

Brad and Tim exchanged a dark look silently.

Carly grinned and tapped his chest. "What? Did you think that the ghost got me? C'mon. It was funny!" She stepped between them. "Let's go up and finish the bottle of wine." She turned and her heels followed a smooth flash of thigh as she sprinted up the steps.

"Quite the sense of humour." Brad rolled his eyes before turning to follow her up to the main floor. With a hand on the stair rail, he turned and added, "But... it *was* kinda funny!" Shaking his head, he continued up the stairs.

Tim's legs felt like rubber as he headed to the stairs. When Carly's motionless body appeared, he *was positive* it was Baxter's revenge for the night before; they had pushed him too hard and he was paying back. What were they thinking? That entity drove not one, but *two* men to slaughter their families, right?

"No! Those men were crazy!" he said out loud. Putting one foot on the stairs he slowly gazed around the room. "Screw you, Baxter," he said in a low voice before ascending.

When he emerged in the hallway, Carly was there with a big grin on her face and holding the Ouija board in her hands.

"Let's try this out. When I wanted to the other night, Tony went all ape shit about it. Let's see if that ghost Baxter will respond." Her eyes were bright and cheeks flushed. Tim was stunned to realize *this was turning her on*!

He looked over at Brad. They were both thinking the same thing. Was Baxter still there, after last night? Brad shrugged.

Tim stepped forward and took the board from her. "Okay, let's give it a go." He looked over to Brad. "We're probably going to get a lot of use out of it when we have paying guests, right? So we may as well have a run through with it beforehand." He turned back to Carly. "You know how this works?"

"Well yeah...duh...of course, I do! What kid hasn't played with one of these?" She looked away from Tim and spoke in a low voice. "I did have an experience once that was kind of spooky." She looked from one to the other and then continued. "One night me and two of my friends were playing with one of these and we started to communicate with a spirit that said it was my dead grandfather." She rubbed the surface of the board. "He passed away before I was born." Still staring at the board, she said, "As a test, I asked him what was his middle name and he spelled it out." She looked up from the board to Tim and Brad. "He spelled out Alphonsus."

"That's an odd name," said Brad.

Carly nodded. "Yeah. I was about ten years old. I had never heard of that name before that night, so I wrote it down." She looked up at the ceiling of the room. "When I asked my mother about it, she told me that yeah, his middle name was Alphonsus."

"Well, you probably just heard it at some time or another and it was in your sub-conscious," said Brad.

Carly gave a quick grin while shaking her head. "Maybe. But I don't think so. I didn't even know 'Alphonsus' *was* a name until I spoke to my mother. If I had heard it before I wouldn't have been surprised, right?"

"Well, it sure isn't a name I would want to have." Brad started to head towards the kitchen. "You guys ready to try this?"

"No, No. Not in *there*! Let's try it in the parlour. It's a pretty creepy spot. I'll bet that's where the ghost hangs out mostly. I'll grab a couple of candles and we'll set it up." Carly pointed to the living room and made a mad dash to the kitchen for the candles and the wine.

When she was gone Tim turned to Brad. "You don't really believe this stuff do you?" Part of him wanted Brad to say no but another part was anxious to see if the house was still haunted. All day, everything had been quiet. Too quiet.

Brad shrugged his shoulders and turned to wander into the parlour. He pulled the coffee table to the centre of the room, and threw some cushions onto the floor around it. "Maybe this will be fun. I'm not sure if it works or not but Tony was sure freaked out about it. So, there might be something to it."

Carly's appeared a few moments later carrying a wooden tray with the wine, glasses and candles spread out on its surface. She set the candles around the room before setting the tray down on the floor.

Tim spread the board on the coffee table and she giggled as she topped up their glasses. "Get the lights Brad, will you?" Her eyes were bright with anticipation. "This is kind of cool, don't you think?"

Tim didn't know what to think. He lowered onto a cushion and gestured for her to pass him a glass of wine. As he took a sip, he looked at both of them over the rim of the glass. If Baxter was still a non-paying resident of the house, he needed some liquid courage. Was it to be a repeat of the previous evening?

Carly cleared her throat and placed her fingertips on the triangular planchette. "C'mon Tim, Brad. Follow my lead."

Tim's hands rose to barely brush against the top of the small, wooden platform. From the corner of his eye, he saw Brad grin and then his fingertips joined the others, resting on the planchette. It was odd but it seemed like the planchette was vibrating under his fingers. Tim took a deep breath and squared his shoulders. "Is there a spirit in this room?"

Carly's eyes flickered from one corner of the room to the next.

The vibration under Tim's fingers increased but the triangle stayed in the same place, not even a hint that it was going to slide to the 'yes' or the 'no' position.

"I can sense a presence in the room. Are you unable to communicate?" Carly looked deadly serious.

Tim had to bite his lower lip to keep from laughing. If Baxter was unable to communicate, how would he be able to answer? Dumb question.

The planchette seemed to fly to the word 'No' on the board. Tim's eyes opened wider and his breath hitched in his throat. No? No what?

"What is your name?" Carly's voice was barely above a whisper, as she strained forward, hovering over the board.

The planchette began to circle in the centre of the board. It was going so fast that Tim's fingers fluttered off the surface and he forced himself to connect again. He glanced over at Carly and Brad. Were they moving it? He shivered, noticing for the first time that the air had suddenly gotten colder. Shadows danced on the walls from the flickering candles.

"Is there something you wish to tell us?" Again, Carly sounded awestruck.

The planchette immediately slid to the letter 'S'. It paused and then in sequence slid quickly to 'O', 'P' and 'H'.

Tim's brows drew together. The planchette once more began to move. His fingers barely managed to keep contact with the small triangle and even Brad's fingers hovered above it a few times. "I' and then an 'E'.

The hair on the back of his neck tingled coldly and his mouth went suddenly dry. 'SOPHIE'?

"What the..." Brad's eyes were wide when he looked over at Tim.

The planchette flew off the board and landed across the room, clattering against the hardwood. Tim flinched at the crash and his eyes flashed over to Brad and Carly. They looked as freaked out as him. There was no way either of them had sent the small triangle shooting off the board.

"Enough! This is bullshit!" Brad got to his feet and stormed out of the room.

Tim's heart was hammering like a piston in his chest. He looked over at Carly. "Did you do that?"

For a moment she looked like an owl, her eyes wide, shaking her head from side to side. "No!" She edged closer to him and her hand clutched his shoulder. "Remember how the cabinets... and the water faucets were open the morning that Sophie was here? There's something about her that makes things get even weirder around here."

Brad stomped back into the room and glared at them, and then around the room with a look of pure venom. He tossed back the rest of the wine in his glass and poured another. Fear battled with anger in his face. His other hand rose and he scooped the crucifix from the neck of his shirt. "Hey Baxter! Nice parlour trick. What do you do for an encore?"

A ball of ice formed in Tim's gut. If they didn't cool it, this was going to get out of hand. He rose and he stood in front of Brad, shaking his head slightly. "No man. Let's just let it go. Don't let it get to you...c'mon—"

Brad shoved him aside and strode over to the library where the rocking chair sat still. He kicked the wooden chair and it slammed over, landing against the wooden shelves with a crash. "Sophie's not part of this, you miserable bastard!"

In an instant, the room was plunged into absolute darkness. The light fixtures, and the candles were all snuffed out in the same instant.

Chapter 24

Brad

Brad was rooted to the spot in the pitch blackness. His rage at this spirit was overwhelmed by his fear of its power. With the snap of its fingers, it was able to turn Brad's world into a black hole. He and Tim thought they could tame this thing?

Oh boy.

A light snapped on for a second across from him when Tim fired up his cell phone and shone it across the room.

Carly used the light to dart to the hallway, Brad turned to watch her and Tim scrabbled to his feet, overturning the coffee table and spilling the Ouija board to the floor.

An ice cold torrent of air whooshed past Brad. It smashed Tim to the floor, and the cell phone rocketed into the wall, shattering into a dozen pieces.

Before the blackness could again register on them, the lights in the upstairs hallways again began to flash. Three short, three long and three short again: SOS.

Booming laughter rolled through Brad. It wasn't coming from anywhere—it was *everywhere*!

"Yes, my pets! Cry out for help! All of you cry out!"

Brad could hear a whimpering from Tim. "Oh shit, man, he broke my wrist!" In the staccato light Tim was lying on his side holding his damaged limb.

"WE HAVE TO GET OUT OF HEEEERE!" screamed Carly. She was at the front door, pulling on it with all her strength to no avail.

"We're coming!" Brad tossed the coffee table aside and lifted Tim up with one hand. "Let's get the hell out of here, man!" Together they stumbled to the door.

Brad shoved Carly aside and yanked on the front door. Nothing moved. The knob refused to turn in his hand, and when he pounded on the slab of the door it didn't budge.

A cackling laugh echoed through him. "Fee Fi Fo Fum! I think Bradley will be the one!"

"He's coming!" screamed Carly. Brad followed her pointing arm and turned towards the staircase.

Backlit by the lights still sending out their plea, they saw Baxter for the first time. He was lightly hopping down the stairs, one at a time. With each step, he transformed. He went from a young man, dressed in a World War II army uniform, to a bearded middle aged man wearing khakis and loafers. The only constant, as each figure morphed into the next was the maniacal grin.

"What do you guys think of my look?" he said, stopping on one step and patting his khakis. "This was all the rage on 911 at the office!"

"Who the hell are you!" Tim demanded. "WHAT the hell are you!"

"Why, I'm Thomas Baxter!" the apparition said and hopped down to the next step. "No, I'm Cory Baxter, Thomas' grand uncle!" said the man in military dress. He hopped to the next step and Thomas Baxter reappeared, his hands shoved into his slacks, leaning back. He pointed to Tim. "And soon, you will be joining us!" Waving at Brad and Carly, he chuckled, "And these two will be joining those already upstairs!" He leaned forward and cocking an eyebrow at Brad, and then Carly, said, "Every night from now until the end of time they relive the terror of their deaths."

"Why?" Carly said, her voice a squeak.

"TO FEED ME!" Baxter shimmered for a moment, replaced by a pulsing swirl of purple and red light. It vanished, and Baxter dropped another step to reform as the soldier.

With a gleeful smile, Uncle Baxter held out his hands. "Shhh now! Listeeeennnnn…" and hopped down a step, morphing back to bearded Thomas.

As the lights flickered on and off, they could hear a series of faint moans and cries. One layered on top of another, occasionally pierced by a far away scream. Thomas's hands rose in the air and the volume of their cries increased.

At the sound of a small child pleading and then ending in a shriek, Baxter's eyes glittered. "That one's my son, just as he begged me not to chop off his other leg, poor lad." He closed his eyes and made a face of orgiastic pleasure. "His is one of my favorites."

He hopped down the step and became Cory Baxter, resplendent in his Army uniform. A young girl's shriek of

'Daddy! Daddy! I can't breathe! Stop it!' floated from the floor above. "I chased her from the house to the dock and drowned her slowly." Cory licked his lips. "Beautiful..." He eyed Carly. "I can't wait to see how you'll match up. A small girl, and a flowered woman... which will be a better meal? Tim loves you, and his smile will be the last thing you see in this life as he drowns you..."

"And you!" he pointed to Brad. "We're going to have a 'Brad-fire' tonight!" Baxter squatted on the step. "I can't wait to watch you writhe after your best friend douses you with gasoline and tosses the match!" Baxter shivered in anticipation, his eyes closed. Opening them, he said, "Okey-dokey, here we go!"

He waved a hand and the three of them froze in place. Brad's feet were welded to the floor. He watched as Baxter came down the rest of the stairs and in horror, approached Tim.

"Hi Tim! How'z it goin'?" Baxter said. He held out his arms. "Give us a hug, *Bro!*" He looked over to Carly as the door to the house swung open with a creak. "You better get going, girl." With a Groucho Marx waggle of his eyebrows he said, "We'll be right behind you!"

Carly flew out the door, shrieking.

Chapter 25

Sophie

From the moment she opened her eyes that morning, Sophie knew this was going to be a Day of Days.

All her life she had been one of those rare people who bounced out of bed, grateful for the gift of a new day. Whether she was hung over, sick with the flu or having a bad period, she always woke up with a sense of gratitude and joy. It drove her parents and her older brother crazy sometimes, but that's the way she was. Even as a baby, when she woke up in her crib, she would lie on her back and sing until Mommy or Daddy came in to get her.

Only once before in her life had she awoken the way she did this day. That day started the same way this day did—she woke up crying.

And that Day of Days was the day her Nana was killed. All the police reports, and even her parents had told her that it was probably a drunk driver that ran off the road, hit her and sent her careening into that oak tree.

Neither the driver nor the car was ever seen nor found.

Sophie had always known it had been murder.

Because Nana told her that night.

Ten years ago, on the night that Nana had died, her spirit came to Sophie. She had been lying in bed crying over poor Nana when in a gentle twinkling of diffused light she was sitting at the foot of her bed.

"Nana!" she cried out reaching to hug her. But her arms went through the old woman's figure. Sophie sat back on the bed and whispered. "You're a ghost?"

Nana nodded. "Yes, dear, this is my spirit. My body has stopped and I'll be moving on soon." Her lips moved, but Sophie didn't hear Nana with her ears, she heard her in her head.

"No, dear, you hear me in your heart."

Sophie's hand went to her breast. "My heart's broken, Nana."

Nana smiled sadly and nodded. "I know. But you'll be safe now. The Beast won't be back for some time. When he returns, you must be ready."

A chill of fear speared the girl. "The Beast?"

Nana nodded. "Yes. He is the dark half of our universe. He feeds on fear and hate. Despair is his dawning joy. Everything you and I hold to be beautiful and good is an abomination to him. Everything he values is anathema to us. It was one of his lackeys that took me from this world today, Sophie."

"Why?"

Nana leaned forward. "To hurt *you*. To take away *your* hope, to drown the fire of joy within you with sadness and despair."

"Me?"

Nana nodded. "You are special, Sophie. So very, very special."

"Why *me*?"

"I don't know, darling. I only know that the Creator has chosen you. You've been protected from the wrath of the Beast by the Creator's angels, and so the Beast took me as a way to hurt you."

"He's *awful*!" Sophie's fists pounded her mattress.

"The Creator's angels have let me return to this plane, but I cannot stay." Nana tried to cup Sophie's face in her hands, but had no more success touching her than Sophie had earlier. "Remember, child, love is eternal. Love will conquer fear. One day you will need to remember that, so remember it well." She stood up and holding her arms out from her waist, she said, "Until we meet again, my dearest Sophie... fare thee well..."

Her voice and figure shimmered and faded, and she was gone.

But she left behind a sense of hope and joy. "Until we meet again, Nana," she said.

This day, she woke as she had *that* day—the tears flowing told her that terrible things were going to happen. She went through her day at work and came home feeling each passing moment of the day weigh heavier and heavier upon her.

Even Aphra had kept her distance from her today, phoning her in the morning to tell her she would be unable to be there.

And for the first time since she began to work there, not a single person came through the door all day. When she left to return home, the streets were empty, too.

When she tried to phone Brad, her phone erupted in static. When she tried to send him a text message, the icon just kept spinning on the screen of her phone, going round and round. She wished she had Tim's number; even though she was sure that she would get the same result.

She considered going out to their Inn... but was too afraid. When she had gone there the first time, the throbbing malignancy that was present was too much to bear.

Coming home she lit incense and tried to meditate, but couldn't empty her mind.

She went to get something to eat, but could only choke down a crust of bread and a small glass of wine.

SOPHIE! IT'S TIME!

It wasn't Nana's voice. It wasn't a voice at all. It was... a *presence*. And in that presence she felt the power of stars a 'borning and the beauty of all that was good. Even so, she shut her eyes tightly. "No! I'm not going out there!"

It's time, Sophie. You have been chosen...

"No! Choose somebody else!" She fell to the floor, prostrate. What the hell did they want from her? She was a store clerk for heaven's sake! She was nothing special! But that... that THING out at the lake... THAT was something 'special'! It made her sick with fear. She lifted her head. "I didn't ask for this! It's not fair!" She got up onto her knees, lifted her face and said, "You need a SWAT team, not a clerk!"

I need YOU. Have faith in ME and in yourself and go.

"But..."

Or they'll all die horribly and will be trapped for millennia!

She struggled to her feet. "But... but..."

Sophie! GO NOW! HURRY! You may already be too late!

She jumped up, put on her sandals and fled out the door.

A moment later she ran back in and grabbed her slouch bag of talismans and charms and fled again.

***

When she had turned off the road to the drive, she saw the lights flickering on and off and knew the signal being sent.

Save Our Souls!

"I'll die trying," she said out loud, then gave a snort. There was an excellent chance that she was going to find out just what was worse than dying, actually. As she grew closer to the house, she could hear the moans of those trapped souls and the cackling laughter of the Beast.

She hadn't heard the *presence* since she left her apartment.

Crap.

After hearing the cries and moans she couldn't turn back though. Damn it.

She had pulled her car right up to the edge of the veranda and jumped out of the car.

At that moment the front door flung open and Carly came running out shrieking. Her hair had turned completely white.

Chapter 26

Carly jumped onto Sophie. "Help meeee! Tim's going to drown me! Help meeee!" Saliva dribbled from the girl and the front of her dress was sodden.

Sophie clutched at the poor girl, holding her. "Fear not, all will be well," she said, not believing a word of it.

From the open doorway of the Inn, terror and despair blasted out in a rage of blue-white light as if it were an explosion, enveloping the two of them in a tumult of hopelessness. Arms entwined, they staggered and tripped back from the house. Carly led them around the large maple tree and hid behind it.

She clutched at Sophie. "We have to run! Run away!"

"Shhh..." said Sophie with a calm she didn't feel as the world around her tumbled. She brought Carly to the side of the property. "Shhh... sit and be well." She lowered the girl to the ground. "I'm going to fetch Brad and Tim now."

Carly stared at her with unfocused eyes. *"You're going back there?"*

Sophie nodded. "I don't have a choice." She raised a hand and pointed at the house. "That *thing* is evil!" She looked at the building, the white and blue light blasting from the doorway. "If it's not stopped, all is lost," she said in an even voice. She looked down at Carly. "Come with me."

"Are you crazy?"

173

With a shrug of her shoulders and a series of quick nods, Sophie said, "Yeah, probably!" She pointed her chin at the house. "But that thing's worse!"

Carly sat back. "I... I don't think I can."

Sophie nodded. "I understand," she said and set off for the doorway.

As she approached the building the air closed in around her, a hundred—no a thousand times worse than when she had first come out to the house. It was so close she gasped as she struggled to put one foot before another.

Staggering, she made it to the steps to the veranda. Everything else had gone deathly quiet. All she could hear were those moans and cries, and even they were muted.

The four steps to the porch could have been a climb to Mt. Everest for all the energy she had left from simply crossing the yard.

She patted the side of her slouch bag and felt the side of the bible she had packed into it.

Nana's bible.

"The Lord is my shepherd," she whispered. A surge of energy shot through her and she put her foot on the stairs. "I shall not want!" she said as she stepped up.

She raise her foot to the next step. "Yea, though I walk through the valley of death!"

She raised her next foot onto the porch. "I SHALL FEAR NO EVIL!"

A hand grabbed her shoulder. "Me neither," said Carly.

Together, holding hands they went into the howling blue-white light, crying out "I FEAR NO EVIL!"

Going through the door, it slammed so loudly behind them it cracked down the middle in two. And a laughter of malevolent glee drowned out their prayer.

Chapter 27

The Beast had shed its skins of Baxter and Baxter and stood before her. Sophie blinked.

"Nana?" she said.

"Oh Sophie, I'm so glad you came!" Nana held out her arms. "Come to me child!"

Leaving a silent Carly behind her, Sophie stepped forward carefully. "Nana?"

With a love she hadn't seen in a decade, her Nana bade her to come. Sophie smiled and her hand went into her slouch bag. She pulled out a plastic water bottle, flipped its lid and doused her Nana with its contents.

"Blessings upon you!" she cried out.

The holy water splashed all over Nana and began to sizzle and pop like an acid bath. She shrieked in agony and grew in size and hate as her flesh fell away. And when Nana was gone, the Beast began to show its true self. It flipped and changed like a slideshow on high speed. From a visage of a cloven hoofed, horned demon to a multi-armed Hindu deity to a Chinese dragon headed man the Beast moved through all of the depictions of evil humanity had created throughout history.

"I fear no evil, I fear no evil," Sophie repeated over and over.

Finally, the Beast stopped its morphing and Sophie gasped, staring at its smile.

She was looking at herself. "How do you like me now, Sophie?" it said. "There's as much of me in you as your 'Lord' is within you." It raised its hand to strike her.

She didn't flinch. She clasped her hands together and said, "May the Lord's will be done." She brought her hands to her lips and closed her eyes. Whatever would now happen would be the will of the Creator. She was summoned here and she held true, but the power that would vanquish this beast was not within her.

She would miss her mornings. "May the Lord send you back where you belong," she said quietly. "For you don't belong here!"

Sophie/Beast hesitated. "No begging for your life?" It smiled at her. "C'mon, give into the fear!"

"His will be done," she said quietly. "I trust in the goodness of the Creator more than I fear you." She wished her knees got that memo— they were knocking together like a snare drum.

In that moment of faith, she felt a power course through her like she had never experienced before. Raising her head, she cried out, "I REBUKE YOU EVIL ONE!" Her voice was the voice of ages, the voice of Joan of Arc, Circe, Durga and Maja, a commanding force that bellowed, shaking the very foundations of the house. Iridescent silken threads sparked through a silvery white aura enveloping her body like armour.

She wouldn't take her gaze away from this entity; they stood facing one another frozen in place.

The moans of the dead had stopped. From the cellar a string of notes tinkled on an out of tune piano.

She knew that tune. *'Frère Jacques, Frère Jacques, Dormez-vous? Dormez-vous?'*

It had a chilling effect on Sophie/Beast. The creature's eyes widened in shock. "No! Back to your cages you!" It looked around wildly.

The Beast's Sophie disguise fell away, revealing a fetid, stinking face dripping mucous and blood from its maw. "FEAR MEEE!" it roared, its voice coming from putrid black depths. But now the thing looked around over its shoulder and up the stairs, fear glimmering in its eyes. Sophie saw children, as greyish orbs, waft down the staircase and encircle the creature, hemming him in. It shrank back from them as it slashed at them with a talon like hand.

Her faith had inspired the children.

In a flash her hand dove into the cloth bag on her shoulder and scrambled inside. Grasping Nana's Bible, a sense of power flowed through her hand.

She gripped it in both hands, twisting her body to hold it high above the beast. Its mouth was snarling obscenities in some ancient foreign language. The creature's eyes changed when it saw what she had in her hands. The straining bulges became guarded narrow slits and its head drew back. The expression on its face became sly, the tongue darting from slippery, wet lips. "I will kill you," it hissed.

Still she advanced up the stairs with the book in her outstretched hands.

"IN THE NAME OF GOD, I COMMAND YOU! GO BACK TO HELL, FILTH!" Sophie smashed the book against the thing's face.

There was a yearning cry that filled the air. Steam carrying the stench of decay, rose above it, the flesh bubbling and searing until there was nothing but a small heap of ashes.

It was over. Sophie let out a sharp gust of air and her shoulders slumped forward, the bible slowly lowering. There was a light touch on her cheeks, like butterfly kisses, the touch was warm and peaceful.

She opened her eyes and the ghostly images of the children were now orbs of white light, rising in the air and fading. The music stopped when they were gone. The feeling of peace and love that she'd felt in their presence evaporated when she looked over at Brad and Tim.

They had both collapsed at the bottom of the stairs. She smiled to herself; they had fainted dead away. Carly was trying to rouse Tim and she clambered over to Brad, putting her ear to his chest. His heart was beating soundly and his breathing was steady.

"We have to get them out of here, Carly!" She rose and stepping next to Carly, each taking an arm they pulled Tim from the house, returned and pulled Brad out.

"Why won't they wake up?" Carly asked.

"They had a terrible fright." Sophie went to the hose reel that was attached to the side of the veranda. Pulling the hose back to them, she sprayed the boys until they sat up, sputtering.

"Get them to the car." She said. Carly began to help Tim to his feet and she returned to the house.

Entering the hallway, she looked around. Everything was quiet now. But it wasn't over. This had been a reprieve, a battle that had been won, but not the war. The evil was gone now, but would return again to this place.

Just as there are sacred places, in this world, she knew there were cursed ones; where it was easy for pure evil to cross into this plane of existence. This house stood on such an accursed plot.

Her cloth slouch bag was on the floor and she reached for it. There was one final thing to do. She took it up stairs and strode into the first bedroom. She pulled out a box of wooden matches and the bundle of sweet grass and herbs. She struck a match and in a moment the dry bundle was aflame. The wallpaper that had been peeled back to reveal the young boy's crayon marks burst into flame above the burning bundle.

Room by room Sophie wandered and set the fires. Still holding the sweet grass bundle, she walked down the stairs. The power of her senses was like a magnet within her, drawing her to the library. She picked up the alchemy book and set it alight. The flames silhouetted her body as she left the room.

Returning outside, she spotted Brad and ran to him. He looked dazed standing in the driveway staring at the house.

"Sophie?"

She nodded. "We have to go. Hurry. The house is burning."

<u>Chapter 28</u>

Brad looked around at the smoke that was just above them, the orange glow in the air. With a lurching stumble, he grabbed for Sophie's hand. She led the way across the driveway to the car where Carly and Tim stood huddled together.

"Oh God." Carly's lower lip trembled as she watched flames engulf the upper floor.

"What happened? Did Baxter set the place on fire? Where is he?" From the look on Brad's face, the reality of what had just happened was hitting him.

Sophie looked at each of the guys—Tim, mutely watching the house, the lights playing over the muscle in his jaw, and Brad, his eyes wide with shock.

"I set the house on fire." Her arms crossed over her chest and she turned to watch the flames consume the building. In an awful way, it was beautiful to see.

"But why? The house... our business?" Brad stepped towards her peering down into her eyes before his shoulders slumped low.

She grabbed his arm and shook it, hard. "Eejit! You're lucky to be alive! You're lucky your soul's not trapped in there flashing the lights on and off!" She took them all in her gaze. "If I didn't come out here, you'd *all* be dead, and reliving the event of your murders every night to feed that... that *Demon's* sick appetite!"

The three of them stared. First at her, then at the house, then at each other.

Tim let out a sharp breath and ran his hand through his hair. "Oh God...I think you got a point there, Sophie."

Sophie nodded at Tim's acquiescence. She turned to Brad. "And could you really let someone else buy the place? Knowing it could happen again?" When he shook his head, she said, "This is an evil spot, period."

"We're going to lose everything.." Brad said, shaking his head.

"No, that's what insurance is for." She folded her arms. "And after you get your settlement, we'll find another place, that's all."

"WHAT?"

It was like Brad and Tim were twins, speaking in unison.

Sophie's hands shot out in exasperation. "Look! It took me a while to come to this, but I have to admit...the idea was not altogether stupid. You just picked the wrong house."

She glared at Brad and Tim. "Next time, ask me to help you, instead of shutting me out. There are *lots* of haunted houses. Benign ones, where the ghosts don't want to kill you! They'll just want to hang out."

Tim looked at her with a newfound respect. "And, I suppose, you're able to tell the difference." When she silently nodded in reply, he said, "No thanks." He looked down at his feet and kicked at a piece of gravel. "I think this is it for me. What we went through tonight makes working at the insurance company look like a cake walk."

"Me too. This was way too scary," agreed Brad. "In fact, I think we would have had a fate worse than death, right Sophie?" Seeing her nod, he continued, "I never really believed in this stuff, until I lived with it." Brad's mouth pulled to the side and he looked down, a long sigh ebbing through his lips.

"*What?* You're willing to give up? Don't get me wrong...you could have been killed and you should have listened to me." She stepped over to Brad and put her arms around his neck, looking up into his eyes."I never realized how much I loved you until I almost lost you."

Tears welled up in her eyes. Everything was hitting her like a wall—the fear and horror of facing that *Beast*. She couldn't bring herself to call it an evil spirit. It was still too fresh. It would totally unnerve her at that point.

Brad's arms went around her and he kissed her forehead. "I know. I love you too."

She pulled back and her hands jabbed at his chest. Ooooo. She loved him yet she was ready to kick him. "In that case, you *really* can't give up. You need me. I'll help you; I'll become a partner. I may not have a university degree but what I've got is a lot more valuable. Think I want to spend the rest of my days working retail for minimum wage? With the talent I have?"

Brad pulled back and his mouth fell open. "What? But you like working at that store. It's all new age and mystical...right up your alley."

Again she jabbed him, harder this time. "Boy! For a so called educated guy, you sure can be dumb. Sure, that stuff is interesting and I enjoy meeting the customers and I like Aphra. But that's no future for me."

This time it was Carly who spoke."What the hell?" She clapped Sophie's shoulder and leaned in to kiss her cheek. "By the way...thanks for saving my life."

Sophie turned to her and smiled. "You're welcome." She looked at Carly's hair. The guys were still too shook up to notice it, but when Carly found a mirror... oh boy.

Before she had a chance to get another word out, Carly spoke again, but this time her words were directed at Tim. "Yeah Tim! You may think you're all of that and a bag of chips but listen....your people skills suck. If you're going to do this again and get a house that's not quite so evil, you need someone with good customer relations skills. Guess who's got tons of experience in the service industry? Me! That's who!"

She turned to Sophie and grabbed her arm. "Hey, if they're too dumb to try this again, why don't you and I go partners? I've got some money saved and there's an inheritance that I'll get next year when I'm twenty-five."

Tim stepped over and pulled Carly to him. "Hey, hey, hey. Un unh. It was our idea and you can't steal it." He led the way to his car pulling her along with him. He turned and spoke once more, looking at Brad and Sophie."We can talk about this tomorrow. For now, Carly and I are going home...to her place."

Sophie stepped close to Brad and slipped her hand into his watching the other couple get in the car and drive up the lane. "I think that's a good idea. Let's blow this popsicle stand." She rose on her tiptoes and kissed his cheek before reaching down to gather her slouch bag. Her grandmother's bible thumped against her thigh and she smiled. There was no doubt who had helped her that night and who would help her in the future.

She'd get Brad and Tim on-side with getting another haunted house. She glanced over her shoulder watching the inferno that the house had become. It was over...for now.

The End

A Note From the Author

Stories of eerie events happening in hotels abound in Kingston. These tales bolster my belief that this city is an uncommon domain where the boundary between realms becomes thin. One such tale I heard—about an inn that was abandoned by its owners because of inexplicable occurrences was the inspiration for this, my second novel of The Hauntings Of Kingston.

Thank you for reading this book. Hopefully, you enjoyed it. If you did, please leave a review on Amazon. Reviews help struggling authors get their books in front of more readers. If for any reason, this book missed the mark for you, please accept my apologies. Hundreds of hours went into its creation and all I can say is "I did my best." If you want to let me know where it fell short, there will be no bad feelings on my part, I promise. I will take your feedback to heart, and try to improve—if not on this one, then certainly on the next.

MICHELLE DOREY

Other Tales of
The Hauntings Of Kingston

Crawley House

The Ghosts of Centre Street

MICHELLE DOREY

Made in the USA
Middletown, DE
30 June 2022

68158207R00109